#3

Trouble at Tumbling Waters

THE MITCHELL BROTHERS SERIES

THE MITCHELL BROTHERS

#3

Trouble at Tumbling Waters

THE MITCHELL BROTHERS SERIES

Brian McFarlane

Fenn Publishing Company Ltd.
Bolton, Canada

TROUBLE AT TUMBLING WATERS
BOOK THREE IN THE MITCHELL BROTHERS SERIES
A Fenn Publishing Book

All rights reserved

The content, opinion and subject matter contained herein is the
written expression of the author and does not reflect the opinion or
ideology of the publisher, or that of the publisher's representatives.

Fenn Publishing Company Ltd.
Bolton, Ontario, Canada

Distributed in Canada by H. B. Fenn and Company Ltd.
Bolton, Ontario, Canada, L7E 1W2
www.hbfenn.com

National Library of Canada Cataloguing in Publication

McFarlane, Brian, 1931-
        Trouble at tumbling waters / Brian McFarlane.

(Mitchell brother series ; 3)
ISBN 1-55168-251-6

        I. Title. III. Series: McFarlane, Brian, 1931 – Mitchell brothers
series ; 3

PS8575.F37T76 2004   jC813'.54   C2004-900756-4

TROUBLE AT TUMBLING WATERS

Chapter 1	To Tumbling Waters	1
Chapter 2	Chased Through the Woods	9
Chapter 3	A Hair-Raising Experience	23
Chapter 4	Learning About Indian Ways	34
Chapter 5	Meeting Susan in the Longhouse	44
Chapter 6	Dealing With Dynamite	53
Chapter 7	The Powwow Begins	62
Chapter 8	The Lacrosse Tournament	71
Chapter 9	Two Tough Competitions	81
Chapter 10	Fire in the Longhouse	93
Chapter 11	Searching for Elmo	104
Chapter 12	The Lacrosse Championship	116
Chapter 13	Banjo Billy Lays Charges	126
Chapter 14	A Visit to Bradley's Valley	135
Chapter 15	Arrested in Silver City	146
Chapter 16	The Jailbreak	161
Chapter 17	The Showdown	171
Chapter 18	Archers Versus Gunmen	181
Chapter 19	A Final Confrontation	193
Chapter 20	Time to Go Home	206

NOTE FROM THE AUTHOR

You may have read in a previous book (*On the Hockey Highway*) about how Max and Marty Mitchell journeyed to an Indian reserve and recruited Sammy Running Fox to play for their junior hockey team, and how the Mitchell brothers decided that the lifestyle and culture of native North Americans was worth exploring.

Fortunately, Sammy's people, the Iroquois, who live in the small village of Tumbling Waters, maintain many of the traditions of the past. They play the exciting Indian game of lacrosse, they display skill with bows and arrows and they enjoy mingling with other native groups at social events called powwows.

Sammy invites Max and Marty to spend some time at Tumbling Waters. He promises them a good time and he tells them of past battles, when his people had to fight for the land they had held for hundreds of years.

What he couldn't have predicted was that they would become involved in a somewhat similar battle with the notorious Blackjack Bradley and his gang of thugs from the nearby town of Silver City.

I hope you enjoy the further adventures of Max and Marty Mitchell in *Trouble at Tumbling Waters*.

Brian McFarlane

ABOUT THIS BOOK

The intent of my workings with Brian McFarlane was to assist in placing his Aboriginal characters in the proper place and historical context. Even though the book is fictional, he was careful to seek out the Aboriginal viewpoint so that the story would be as credible as possible. In my view, it is an honourable effort on his part at incorporating an Aboriginal community into the escapades of the Mitchell brothers.

Ironically, Brian spends part of the year at his summer home near my First Nation community. So, by natural instinct, he sought out from our administration office a person who could assist in reviewing his piece. Having grown up as a Montreal Canadiens fan, with McFarlane as the centrepiece of "Hockey Night in Canada," I jumped at the opportunity.

In my view, it is important that writers and readers of all backgrounds cross over in an attempt to understand each other's communities and backgrounds as McFarlane has attempted. He probably never had a choice but to understand, once I finished scribbling my "marginal notes" from one side of his manuscript to the other. Let me say he took my constructive criticisms and comments well, and I once again thank him and the publisher for the opportunity to be involved.

Dave Mowat
Alderville First Nation, Ontario

PREFACE

There is still no universally accepted term for the peoples native to North America. "Indian," "American or Canadian Indian," "Native American or Native Canadian," "Native Peoples" and "Aboriginals" are all in use but in the opinion of many are not entirely satisfactory terms for identifying the diversity of tribal nations in North America. The native people in our story often called themselves "Anishinabe."

In this book, the word "Indian" is used with the utmost respect and with the expectation that most Native Peoples will not be offended by the use of it.

The author wishes to thank Mr. David Mowatt of the Alderville First Nation in Roseneath, Ontario, for his guidance and expertise on Indian life.

Brian McFarlane

CHAPTER 1

TO TUMBLING WATERS

The old car, a 1927 DeSoto, slowed down as it entered the outskirts of the mining town. Sammy Fox was at the wheel and he turned to his passengers, Max and Marty Mitchell.

"This is Silver City, guys. The Sheriff here loves to hand out speeding tickets, so I always make sure to stay under the limit."

Brothers Max and Marty Mitchell were on their way to Tumbling Waters, an Indian reserve in a remote section of the wooded North Country. Their friend, Sammy Fox, had invited them to spend a few days learning about Indian ways and customs. "It's a special village," Sammy had told them. "Built just like the ones our ancestors lived in for hundreds of years. It's the only place I know where you'll see the old customs and traditions."

"Will we sleep in a teepee?" Max asked.

"No, teepees were home to the Plains Cree—the

buffalo hunters. You'll sleep in a longhouse," he had promised. "In the old days, some of our people lived in wigwams or lodges. In our village, you'll get to play lacrosse, our native game, and take part in a big powwow. You'll be able to shoot arrows from a bow. And paddle a birch bark canoe. Be sure to bring your dog, Big Fella, with you."

In recent months, Sammy, a young Iroquois whose Indian name was Running Fox, had become a close friend to the Mitchell brothers. During the previous winter, Max had recruited Sammy to play on the Indian River hockey team. Max, as player coach, had recognized Sammy's skills as a skater and scorer. Together they had led the club to the junior championship.

Sammy slowed the DeSoto to a crawl. He looked in the rear-view mirror and saw that Marty was squirming in the back seat. Big Fella was asleep on the seat beside him.

"What's the matter, Marty? Got ants in your pants?" asked Sammy.

"Sorry, fellows, but I have to go to the bathroom," Marty blurted. "Real soon." At 15, Marty was two years younger than his brother Max. He had a head of reddish-brown hair.

"I can pull over and you can go behind those bushes," Sammy said. "There's not much activity on the main street today."

"A bush isn't going to help, I need a real bathroom," Marty said, squeezing his eyes shut. "Let's go in the place up ahead. There must be a bathroom in there."

"That's a tavern, Marty," said Sammy. "It's where the Bradley men hang out. You two can go in, and I'll wait in the car with Big Fella."

"But why?" Marty asked. "It's been a long trip. Don't you have to go?"

"Yeah, I do, but..."

"But what?"

"Marty, look at my skin. My black hair. I'm an Indian. I'll be blunt—the Bradleys don't like Indians. So I avoid them whenever I can. You go in with Max. I'll park around the corner and wait for you there. If one of the Bradleys stumbles on me, I've got Big Fella to protect me."

Cautiously, Max and Marty entered the tavern. It was dark inside and Max almost kicked over a bucket of soapy water sitting just inside the door. A woman, thin as a hockey stick, with stringy red hair, was mopping the floors.

"Beg your pardon, ma'am. Do you have a men's room?" Max asked politely.

"You gotta buy somethin'," she snapped. "Otherwise, it's off limits. Customers only." The soapy mop brushed close to their feet and the boys took a step back.

"Sure, I guess we could buy something," Max said. "A couple of soft drinks, please. No, make it three. We've got a friend outside in the car."

She nodded and put down the mop. Her attitude softened when she took a closer look at the teenager. He appeared to be about 17 and tall for his age. He had blond hair, a well-muscled body, good manners and a winning smile. *Now if I was 17 again, instead of 44,* she thought. *If I was young and pretty like I used to be, I'd lock the tavern door and keep this one as a pet.*

She turned to the kid brother. He was shorter and stockier than the blond teenager. *A couple of years younger,* she guessed, *with a pleasant face.*

They look like good kids, she thought. *Well mannered. Younger than my two—Bart and Hugo—and not nearly so wild.*

"Back that way—the men's room."

Marty thanked her and hurried off.

The woman went behind the counter and brought back three soft drinks. She popped off the caps and slipped a container of straws along the bar.

Just then, a burly man wearing a dirty shirt emerged from the kitchen behind the bar. He growled at the woman, "There's an old DeSoto parked at the side."

She shrugged. "So?"

He gave her a dark look. "So? So... there's an Indian at the wheel. Why don't those people stay on the reserve where they belong?"

He looked over at Max, who was busy inserting straws into the pop bottles.

"I haven't seen you in here before," he said. "Where you from?"

"Indian River."

"Say, you look about the same age as the mutt in the car outside. You're not with him, are you?"

Max stammered, "Well, I... what car is that, sir?"

"Don't play dumb with me, fella. If you're a pal of that Indian outside, you can take your drinks and get out. We don't serve their kind here and we don't serve their friends, either."

Marty returned from the restroom and stood next to his brother. He looked puzzled. "What's going on?" he whispered.

"Nothing," Max said quietly. "Come on. Let's go."

They started toward the door when the burly man moved from behind the bar and blocked their path.

"You used the bathroom, kid?" he asked Marty.

"Yes, sir, I did."

"Then you owe me an extra 25 cents."

"What?"

"You heard me. Service charge. Use of bathroom. Gimme a quarter."

"That's ridiculous," protested Max. "You must be kidding."

"I ain't kiddin'," the man snarled. "Your pal used

my toilet paper. Washed his hands with my soap. Gimme 25 cents."

"But I bought three drinks," Max said. He nodded at the red-headed woman. "She said if we bought something..."

"Don't matter what she said," the man barked, pointing at his chest. "I'm the boss of this place." He was turning red in the face. "I want a quarter." He took a step toward them. "Fork it over!"

Max and Marty didn't move.

"Okay. That's it then. Guess I'll have to turn one of you runts upside down and see how much money falls out of your pockets and hits the floor."

His arm shot out and he grabbed Marty by the shoulder in an iron grip.

Marty cried out.

But his cry lasted only a moment. Max sprang forward and struck the man on the forearm with a blow that turned the man's arm to jelly. He howled in pain and released his grip on Marty.

"Run for the door, Marty!" Max ordered.

Obediently, Marty bolted toward the door. But halfway through it, he stopped and doubled back quietly. He crouched down behind the man who was directing his rage at Max.

"Now I'm going to give you a serious beating, you mutt."

The man raised his huge fists. But before he could

lash out with them, Max darted in close, in between the man's heavy arms. Using both hands, he shoved hard on the man's chest. The man howled in surprise. He flew backwards over the kneeling Marty and landed hard on the tavern floor. His head struck the mop bucket, then bounced off the floor. Dirty water flew out of the bucket, sloshing over his face. He lay there, dazed and semi-conscious. Soapsuds drooled from his mouth.

Max and Marty started toward the door. "Wait a second," Max said. "I paid for the drinks." He went back and swept the three bottles off the bar.

"Thanks for the drinks, ma'am," he called out. "Tell your boss our fee for the... uh... entertainment is 25 cents. That offsets his bathroom fee, so I guess we're even."

"He's not my boss," the red-headed woman snapped. "He's my husband—Blackjack Bradley. Don't you know he owns this town? You two better git before he comes around."

"Then we'd best get along," Max said brightly. "Please thank your husband for his kind hospitality. It's not often that mutts like us meet a man who'll bend over backwards for us."

Marty giggled before adding, "He was just as nice as Santa Claus. Tell him I'm sorry I used all of his toilet paper. I'll bring him a roll next time we come to visit." Marty looked thoughtfully at the man on the floor.

"Or maybe tough guys like him prefer sandpaper."

"Smart alecks," the woman snorted. "Get on out of here."

When the Mitchell brothers left the tavern and roared off in the DeSoto with Sammy, the woman was watching from a window. Her face broke into a smile. *That good-looking blond kid showed Blackjack up big time. He'll probably pay a high price for it one day. But the kid had spunk. And charm. And a winning personality.* She thought, *Oh, to be 17 again.*

CHAPTER 2

CHASED THROUGH THE WOODS

The Mitchell brothers ran swiftly along the narrow path, a sandy route that snaked its way through the deep woods. Max Mitchell led the way, moving over the ground with long, graceful strides. Marty, less agile and with shorter legs, was breathing hard as he tried to keep up. Max leaped over a fallen log, took a few paces and stopped. He turned and grabbed his brother by the arm as Marty bumped into him from behind. Max put his fingers to his lips.

"Hush! I thought I heard noises up ahead," Max whispered. "It might be water in the creek, or it could be someone waiting to pounce on us."

"Or it could be a bear," Marty whispered, his eyes wide. "A mother bear with cubs. We were warned to watch out for her. We'll be goners. She'll eat us alive."

"I don't think it's a bear," Max said in his brother's ear, speaking so quietly that Marty strained to hear him. "It may be the Indians who've been chasing us. Some of them may have circled in front of us. They know these woods a lot better than we do. Remember, if they find us before sundown, they'll take our hair."

Marty's face turned a sickly colour. "I thought we'd left those Indian boys miles behind. Now what are we going to do?"

"First, we're going to erase our tracks. We're being chased by some of the best trackers in the North Country." Max snapped a branch off a nearby cedar tree and brushed over the footprints they'd left on the path—erasing them all the way back to the fallen log.

"Good job, brother," said Marty. "They'll think we ran along the log and into the bush."

Max threw the cedar branch aside. "Quick! Follow me!" he ordered, "And be quiet." Max slipped into the dense woods and disappeared. Marty followed, grabbing Max by the shirttail so they wouldn't get separated. The boys moved silently through a grove of maple and birch trees, and came upon the slope of a deep ravine flanked by cedars and pines.

"Climb on my back, Marty," Max said, breathing heavily.

"But why?" Marty asked. "I'm not so tired I can't keep up with you."

"It's not that," Max answered. "If they follow our footprints—and they will—seeing one pair of tracks may fool them. They'll think we split up and went in different directions."

Max hoisted his brother up on his back and moved along the edge of the ravine. When he came to a rock-filled gully leading down the slope of the ravine, he lowered his brother to the ground.

"Climb down the rocks, Marty. That way you won't leave any prints. When you get to the stream, put some wet mud on your face. Your pale skin stands out like a beacon."

"Aren't you coming, Max? Don't leave me down in that ravine. I've lost all sense of direction."

"I'll join you in a minute. I'll run a few yards farther, leaving some obvious footprints. Then I'll double back through the trees."

A small creek flowed through the ravine. When Max slipped down the steep slope, the boys splashed into the water. But they didn't go straight to the other side.

"We'll make our way downstream," Max said. "Then we'll slip up the far bank through some bushes. We've got to make it difficult for anyone to follow our tracks."

Before leaving the stream, Max paused to scoop up some mud. He buttered his face and neck with it. Marty giggled. "Now we both look like raccoons."

When they reached the top of the far side of the ravine, they came upon an open field. In places, large rocks popped up from the ground as if daring any farmer to uproot them, or even work a plough around them. Charred tree stumps lay everywhere, but there were places where tall weeds and grasses flourished, some of them almost shoulder high.

"A forest fire's been through here," Max murmured. "But years ago. A lot of the trees have grown back."

"But not enough to keep us hidden," Marty replied, a worried look on his face.

"Then keep down," Max whispered, yanking Marty by the hand and leading him through the grass toward a sizeable rock formation that shot up in the middle of the field. There was a small weather-beaten wooden shed perched up against a vertical wall of rock.

"Let's take a look," Max said.

They approached the tumbledown shed, which was obviously deserted. Over the open door was a sign in faded print: North Country Silver Mine: 1906. Danger! Keep Out!

"We can hide in the shed," Marty exclaimed. "The door's wide open."

"Hmmm. I don't think so, Marty. Those young Iroquois chasing us will know about this mine. But if I go inside, then back out leaving two sets of prints pointing toward the shaft..."

"They'll think we went down in the mine," Marty

blurted. He peered through a window covered with cobwebs. "There's no back wall to this shed. Just a big hole that must lead to the mine shaft."

They did as Max suggested. While Marty waited impatiently, Max left footprints that led through the shed and into the dark mouth of the mine. Then, walking backward, he left another set of prints next to the ones he'd just made.

"Looks good," Marty said approvingly. "They'd fool me."

"They might not fool an expert tracker," Max said. They hurried away, leaving the door open, exactly as they'd found it.

"There's a pile of rocks over there," Marty said, pointing at an outcropping several hundred yards away. "Maybe we could hide behind them."

"Okay," Max answered. "Those rocks appear to be right on the border of the Indian reserve. We'll move fast and keep low."

After Max circled the rocks, he turned to Marty, a grin on his face. He pointed down. "Look! Some animal has dug a big hole under this rock. It's a cave— a perfect hiding place."

"I'm not going into that hole," Marty protested. "There may be a man-eating bear hibernating in there."

Max said, "Marty, it's summer. Bears don't hibernate in summer."

"Maybe the bear went in there to take a nap. Too bad Big Fella isn't with us. He could go in first and check it out."

Big Fella was their prize husky. Earlier that day, before they'd raced away from Tumbling Waters and into the woods, they'd used a long leash to tie Big Fella to a tree. Two young Indian boys promised to look after him.

"Marty, if there was a bear living in that hole we'd see some tracks, some poop maybe. Do you see any? Well, neither do I. Let's go. We'll hide in there until the six o'clock deadline." He looked around at the deepening shadows. "That should be less than an hour. Come on. I'll go first."

The brothers crawled into the small cave until only their heads could be seen at the entrance. Max pulled some of the tall grass away from the soil and propped it up in front of their hideaway.

"I'll put some loose rocks in the opening," Marty said. "They'll help hold those shoots of grass in place." He scooped up some small rocks and lined them up. "Hey, that's a pretty one," he added, turning a rock over in his hand. "Think I'll keep it." He slipped the rock in his pocket.

"We should be safe now," Max said confidently. "They'll never find us here. Looks like our hair is safe for another day, brother."

Marty ran a hand over his head. "My hair is my

best feature," he said with a small grin. "I'd like to keep it a while longer."

It had been five hours since they'd scampered away from the Indian village. At noon, old Chief Echo, in his deerskin robe, his many necklaces, his feather headdress, holding tight to his mysterious medicine pouch, had addressed them in front of the villagers. "As Sammy's friends, you are welcome here. Sammy says you are willing to take part in one of our oldest traditions—a friendly game of chase and seek. Do you accept the challenge?"

Max looked over at Sammy, who smiled and nodded.

"Yes, Chief Echo," answered Max. "We accept the challenge."

"Good," said the Chief. "When I shout 'Run!' you will run like rabbits. I will give you a ten-minute head start. Then my young scouts, led by Elmo Swift, will come after you. They will track you down. Surely take you prisoner." He laughed and slapped his thigh. "And then try to hold on to your hair."

"Hold on to our hair? Take our hair?" Marty howled. "You're not serious, are you? You said it was a friendly game."

The villagers laughed and chattered among themselves.

The old Chief held up one arm and the crowd was silent.

"If you hide from our scouts until six o'clock, you will win the game. You will be rewarded," he said. "And your hair will be safe."

A husky young man had moved close to Max and Marty while the Chief was speaking. He nudged Max in the ribs with an elbow and scowled at him.

"I'm Elmo Swift," he said belligerently. "Sammy says you are fast—a good athlete. I am fast, too. And I know every inch of this reserve. I will catch you personally. And catch you quickly. Within an hour. Two at most."

Max smiled at Elmo. "I see you take this game seriously, my friend."

"I am not your friend," Elmo snarled. He puffed out his chest. "This year I was named 1936 athlete of the year for this reserve." He spat on the ground and grinned at them slyly. "If I don't catch you, maybe the man-eating bear will. A mean old mother bear with cubs." He motioned toward the nearby trees. "She's out there somewhere. She roams these woods." Then he turned and walked away.

"I think you're just trying to scare us, Elmo." Max shouted after him. "Nice try."

Before Marty could utter one of his customary flippant remarks, like, "Hey, Elmo, who do you think you're talking to?" Max clapped a hand over his brother's mouth, spun him around and pushed him toward the start of the trail. "No time to lose," he said. "The old Chief just shouted 'Run!' He means business. Move your butt!"

As though they were fleeing a burning building, the brothers sprinted down the trail.

Max was a brilliant runner. Back home in Indian River, he'd won the annual marathon race in record time. Sammy Fox once said of Max, "He could shoot an arrow from a bow and run so fast the arrow would land behind him. I do believe he can run as fast as he can skate."

But outstanding speed would not help Max on this day. Because Marty was slower afoot and couldn't keep pace, Max would have to resort to his wits and his guile if the brothers hoped to frustrate Elmo Swift and the other pursuers.

Now the brothers were hunkered down, almost invisible to the outside world as the sun drifted behind the tall trees, making long shadows across the swaying grass.

"Why does Elmo dislike us so much?" Marty whispered. "What did we ever do to him?"

"Don't take it personally," Max whispered back. "I think he's bitter because 500 years ago, white people took the land away from his people—the Indians."

"Come on. That's ancient history. Nothing to do with us."

"Look at it from Elmo's viewpoint. Our forefathers—the English, French and other Europeans—came here and pushed the Indians farther and farther inland. If the Indians resisted, they were killed. If they made peace, their tribes were often ravaged by diseases like smallpox, brought here by our ancestors."

"I guess you could blame Christopher Columbus then," Marty said. "Didn't he start it all?"

"Actually, the Vikings discovered North America long before Columbus. But he gets all the credit. My history teacher says Columbus never touched the shores of North America but stayed on an island miles to the east."

"Was he a good guy?"

"My history teacher? He's all right. Gives a lot of homework."

Marty punched him on the arm. "Not him, you birdbrain. I meant Columbus. And you know it."

Max grinned. He liked to tease his brother. He said, "The people who lived here first don't think so. When Columbus came back a second time, with 1,000 soldiers, he set up a colony and enslaved the Taino Indians. They were forced to work for the Spaniards who went looking for gold. They murdered and looted and brought their diseases." He shrugged.

"Gee, I always thought he was a hero," Marty said. "Most people say he discovered America. First man here and all that. They even have parades for him every year."

"Goes to show. You can't believe everything you read in the paper."

"You can in Dad's paper," Marty said, referring to their father. Harry Mitchell owned the *Review*, the only newspaper in their hometown of Indian River.

Max shifted his weight. Several small pebbles rolled away from the opening.

"I've got a chocolate bar with me," Marty said. He pulled the Oh Henry from his pocket and shared it with Max. They drank from a canteen of water Max had clipped to his belt.

"Make sure the Oh Henry wrapper is tucked away in your pocket." Max said. "We'll leave no signs we've ever been here."

"I think it's cooling off," said Marty. "I've stopped sweating."

He farted and giggled.

"Hush!" said Max. "We'd better be quiet."

Several minutes passed. It was almost six o'clock, almost sundown. Max sniffed the air, then turned to glare at his brother.

"Did you just fart again?" he asked.

"Just a little one," Marty snickered. "One of my famous quiet ones. Remember, we had beans last night."

Max pinched his nose with two fingers. "Whew.

A skunk would run for cover if he met you on the trail. I'm going to get up and take a look around. It's almost six o'clock. Looks like we've won this little game."

"I'll look, too. Four eyes are better than two."

The brothers pushed the grass barrier aside and slowly got to their feet.

"Eeeee-yowwwww!"

The blood-curdling scream came from the throat of Elmo Swift. It caused both the Mitchell brothers to jump in surprise and fear. Before they could react, they were tackled from behind. Elmo Swift and several Indian boys had crept stealthily up to their hiding place. They had been waiting patiently for the Mitchells to make a move. The brothers hadn't heard so much as a whisper, neither the soft squish of a moccasin stepping on a twig nor the sound of a dislodged pebble rolling along a rock. They were taken completely by surprise.

Big hands closed over their mouths. Other hands pulled their arms behind their backs. Deerskin bags with small air holes in them were thrown over their heads. Max heard the voice of Sammy Fox call out. "Don't be too rough on them, Elmo. They're my friends."

Elmo Swift snorted angrily. "They are not my friends. They hide in holes like scared gophers. They almost won contest. Makes us look bad."

The last thing Marty saw, or *thought* he saw, was a huge black bear, standing upright and howling in anger. He yelped in fear. Then the bag slipped over his eyes and he could see no more.

"Eeeee-yowwwww! Eeee-yowwww!"

The brothers were pulled roughly through the long grass and led back to the village. They were stunned and shaken by the ambush and surprised that they'd been captured only minutes from the deadline. Marty, his heart beating wildly, was worried about the black bear he'd seen. Or had he imagined it?

That image put Marty on the verge of tears. "I wish you'd never brought me to this dern place, Max," he muttered. But his voice was muffled and Max didn't hear.

"Did you say something, Marty?"

Marty all but shouted into the deerskin covering his face. "Yeah, I said this was a terrible idea, coming to this Indian place. Now we may lose our hair."

"Well, some of us lose our hair when we get older, anyway," Max replied. "With us it may be sooner than we expected."

Marty couldn't believe his brother sounded so unconcerned. "You're not funny, Max. This is pretty scary, you know. That old bear is going to chew me up and spit out my bones."

"What old bear?" Max asked. "I didn't see a bear."

"Well, I did. And he was licking his lips and drooling when he looked at me. He had more teeth than an alligator. And he was blacker than a crow in a cave. He looked at me like he wanted to open me up to see what's inside."

Elmo Swift moved close to the Mitchells and hissed at them. "You boys were caught before sundown. Fart smells gave you away. Now get ready to pay price."

CHAPTER 3

A HAIR-RAISING EXPERIENCE

The Mitchell brothers and their captors arrived back in the village of Tumbling Waters. All of the inhabitants gathered around and cheered the young Iroquois who'd been involved in the capture. The Mitchell brothers were greeted with a mixture of taunts and cheers. "Caught like wild turkeys," someone shouted. "Now you lose your feathers."

"And your hair," someone else reminded them.

"Leave them alone," another voice demanded. "They were hard to catch. Another two minutes and they'd have won the contest. They almost made Sammy and Elmo look foolish."

Old Chief Echo heard the commotion. He made his way out of the longhouse wearing a colourful headdress and a long beaded deerskin coat. Women and children threw more wood on the fire that blazed in the centre of the village, sending sparks and spirals of smoke skyward.

Under their hoods, Max and Marty could hear the snap and crackle of burning tree limbs and logs. They could hear the sizzle of flames searing roasted flesh.

"We're goners for sure," Marty cried out. "They're gonna cook us and eat us."

Max uttered a terse response. "No they're not. Be quiet."

The two captives were pulled close to the fire and ordered to drop to their knees.

Only then were the deerskin bags pulled off their heads.

Seated directly in front of them was the old Chief. Grey hair shot out from under his red headband. In his gnarled hands he held a long wooden staff. His stern countenance gave way to a wicked grin. Max and Marty noted the absence of several front teeth.

Slowly he poked the staff at Max, touching him in the stomach.

"You boys caught fair and square by my trackers, Blondie." The reference was to Max's mop of tousled hair, bronzed by the summer sun. He pointed to the west. "Caught you before the sun dipped over horizon, right?"

"That's right, sir. Before six o'clock. But only minutes before. And if my brother hadn't broken wind..."

"Still, you lose." The Chief shrugged. Before you

ran away, we promise to catch you before sundown. We do that, right?"

"Yes, sir. That's fair."

The old Chief turned his cunning eyes on Marty. His staff snaked out and tapped Marty on the breastbone, almost knocking him on his backside.

"And you, little bean eater. The one who farts. You not run like your brother, the rabbit. You slower than a snail with sore feet. You know what's coming to you now?"

Marty cast his eyes toward the campfire. "You're not cannibals, are you?" he croaked.

The old Chief cackled and slapped one knee with his hand.

"No, no, little tortoise," he cried out. He pointed his staff toward the fire. "That wild pig on the spit will be our dinner tonight." He patted his stomach. "Besides, your meat may not be good for Chief's digestion. Your meat probably tough. Bitter too. Need plenty of ketchup." The villagers laughed and clapped their hands. Chief Echo grinned, amused by his own wit. He turned away and spat something— it looked like tobacco juice—on the ground.

The news that Marty wasn't going to be the main course on the evening menu didn't quell his fears. "Then I bet you're going to sic that mangy old bear on us," Marty exclaimed, looking the old Chief directly in the eyes, trying hard not to blink.

"Mangy old bear?" the Chief answered. "I'll show you mangy old bear."

The old Chief signalled with his fingers, and from among the onlookers a peculiar-looking bear sprang into view. It hobbled toward Marty and then rose up on its hind legs. It waggled its front paws and a mighty roar came from somewhere inside its huge head.

Marty recoiled, frightened. And yet—and yet—he knew something wasn't quite right with the bear.

Just then, the head of the bear fell from its body and almost landed in Marty's lap. He leaped back. Then the bearskin was thrown aside and fell at the feet of the laughing young man who'd been wearing it. Marty's mouth flew open and he grew red in the face. He'd been frightened to death by a kid posing as a bear. It was humiliating. He managed a grin but found it hard to laugh along with the villagers who greatly enjoyed his discomfort. They applauded the young man for making an old bearskin come to life.

Before Marty could fully recover, the young fellow pulled a long knife from a sheath on his hip.

He approached the Mitchell brothers. "Great Chief says you must pay price now. Here goes. Ready or not."

In an instant, he gripped Marty by his red hair and his knife flashed out. Marty tried to pull back, crying, "Wait a dern minute..." But it was too late.

The Indian held a small clump of Marty's hair in his hand. Then he turned to Max and repeated the act. Now he held up two small clumps of hair. "These haircuts free—on the house," he said, laughing. "Next time you pay me 25 cents."

He turned to the Great Chief, who took the hair and swiftly tied each clump to his long staff, using a leather thong to hold the hair in place. He held the staff above his head and, in a singsong voice, spoke words in his tribal language. Max and Marty didn't understand any of it.

The old Chief then walked to the blazing fire and held the staff to the flames. The hair was quickly burned off the staff. He turned and approached the Mitchell brothers. When he spoke, to their surprise, he no longer talked in half sentences, like the Indians in the Hollywood movies they'd seen. "We sacrifice this human hair—your hair—to the Gods we honour and believe in. In the old days, when we were known as wild Indians or savages, the white man's entire scalp might be taken as a symbol of victory. But now the wars between white men and red men are over. No longer do we chase and kill each other.

"Today, however, we relive the past with a game of chase and seek. But it was just a game, nothing more. We thank you, Max and Marty, for being good sports, for playing our game with skill and for offering your gift of hair."

"We didn't exactly offer," Marty whispered to Max.

"Chief Echo is very articulate," Max observed. "Not like before. Before he was playing a role, like the Indians in the movies. They all were. The Chief probably speaks several tribal languages, as well as English."

The Chief continued. "We hope the same Gods who give us good crops and good hunting will smile on your small sacrifice of hair today. And bring you good fortune in the future."

Max surprised Marty by saying, "Hi-ne-a-wah. Chief Echo. You do us a great honour."

Marty murmured so only Max could hear. "That was good, Max—what you said. Sounded like hyena. What's it mean?"

"It's a simple thank you. Sammy taught me how to say it."

"Well, it impressed me. Listen! I lost more hair than you did, brother. Maybe my good fortune will be to discover a gold mine someday. Or win the Stanley Cup."

"And maybe you'll become King of England, too," was Max's hushed response.

"I could handle that," Marty whispered. "I'd look good in a crown."

"You may get crowned here and now if you're not careful," Max retorted.

The old Chief motioned to someone in the crowd of onlookers to come forward.

"Now I call on Sammy Running Fox, who invited the Mitchell brothers to our village. Sammy will finish this ceremony. I'm tired. I'm going to take a nap before dinner." The old man turned and went to the longhouse. He stopped at the entrance, looked back and winked.

Marty nudged Max. "Did you see that, Max? The old guy winked at me. And he grinned at me. This whole day has been—has been—wild, hasn't it?"

"You might call it surreal."

"And I might not call it surreal because I don't know what surreal means."

"It means—well, I think it means—an oddly dreamlike state. Anyway, the day has been a challenge, a trial for us. The tribe members wanted to test our skills in the woods and our endurance. All things considered, I think we did pretty well. You didn't really think anyone was going to scalp you, did you? Or a bear would get you?"

"Of course not," Marty fibbed. "Mind you, I was a little bit concerned when they captured us. That fake bear kinda worried me. But then I decided to play along just like everybody else. You know, humour them, and pretend I was scared. But it wouldn't have hurt you to tell me that this day was all in fun. I almost wet my pants when those Indians jumped on us outside that rock."

Max laughed and said, "I guess I forgot to tell you. Besides, our hosts wanted to see how well you stood up to a little stress. You did very well."

By then their friend Sammy was pulling Max and Marty to their feet.

Sammy led the villagers in a round of applause for Max and Marty. One native youth beat a tattoo on a leather drum.

Sammy called for silence. It was obvious he held everyone's respect.

"My people!" he began. "Today our young visitors were tested in our ways. And they passed the test. They showed stamina and initiative. On the trail, they backtracked and wiped out their footprints. For a time, we thought they had split up. That's when Max carried Marty on his back. Then we thought they were hiding in the abandoned silver mine. We might never have caught them. But they made one or two little mistakes."

"What mistakes?" Marty asked.

Sammy explained. "We were about to give up when I remembered seeing a broken branch along the trail—a small one from a cedar tree. I said to Elmo, 'Let's go back. Cedar branches just don't break off by themselves.' Sure enough, we picked up your trail and followed you to the stream where you were clever enough to exit the water many yards from where you entered it. After that, we were almost fooled into thinking you'd gone through the shed and down into the mineshaft. Then I bent down and took a closer look at your footprints and saw you'd retraced your steps. And when you hid in the cave we couldn't see your faces because they were covered in mud. That was also very clever. I congratulate you."

Sammy Running Fox turned back to his people. "Folks, this game of chase and seek has been played by our people for over a hundred years. The Mitchell brothers are the first in the memory of the Great Chief to elude our hunting party for so long—right up until sundown. They deserve our respect and they've earned the right to be named honorary Iroquois braves. Don't you agree?"

The villagers cheered and applauded. Many came to shake Max and Marty by the hand and pat them on the back. But one villager was not so complimentary. Elmo Swift went nose-to-nose with Max and told him bluntly, "I am the strongest and fastest teenager here. The best wrestler and the best lacrosse player. Everybody knows it. I wanted to block up your hiding place with big rocks and leave you there to starve. But Sammy wouldn't let me."

Max bristled. "I guess that's why Sammy is so well respected and you're the rotten apple in the barrel," he said, staring Elmo straight in the eye.

"Why don't you and your milk-skin brother go

back to Indian River where you belong?" Elmo hissed. "You are soft white boys. You don't deserve to be honorary members of this tribe. I wish my people had really scalped you."

Before Max could reply, Elmo Swift stalked away.

But Sammy overheard and apologized to Max.

"Elmo Swift has a lot of problems, Max. He's got no friends, no family except for a brother. He's jealous of you. He's jealous of me, too. Try to ignore him. I'm sorry he came up to you. I should have stopped him."

"That's okay," replied Max, gripping Sammy by the shoulder. "At least he was truthful. Now I know how he feels about me—about white men. We'll keep our eyes open when he's around."

"Sammy, do you have any old football helmets we could borrow?" Marty asked, running a hand through his thick hair. "I worry when Elmo talks about scalping people."

Just then, the young native who'd worn the bear suit, scaring Marty almost out of his underwear, came over to meet the Mitchell brothers. No longer did he speak in a menacing voice. Nor did he use words like "No more talk. Just move. Scalpers are waiting."

In perfect English, he said, "Way to go, fellows. Welcome to our village. My Indian name is Black Bear. No surprise, right? But you can call me Johnny

Black. Say, you two were the toughest pair we've ever tried to capture. It took us hours and we would have had to give up at six o'clock. You should be proud of yourselves."

Sammy, meanwhile, had produced a pair of headbands; each equipped with the feather of a hawk. He placed the bands on the heads of the Mitchell brothers.

"I'm proud of you both and I hope you're proud of yourselves," Sammy said.

"Well, I guess we are proud," Marty answered. "I'm just happy the whole thing was just a game."

"And it was a game in which you stood up to rough handling and intimidation. You were smart and brave and very elusive. What's more, the Great Chief has given you new names."

"He has? What are they?"

"From now on, Max will be called Flying Hare because of his great speed afoot."

"What about me?" Marty asked. "What's my new name?"

Sammy laughed and said, "The Great Chief says to call you Puny Turtle."

CHAPTER 4

LEARNING ABOUT
INDIAN WAYS

On the following day, Great Chief Echo once again held court, this time outside the longhouse. The many villagers gathered around, chatting quietly with one another until the Chief raised his hand and called for silence.

"I have wonderful news," he began. "Five other tribes have accepted our invitation to have a huge powwow. The powwow will take place here on our very own reserve next week. It will be the highlight of the year 1936. Many of our brothers from other tribes are already en route, for it will take them many days to get here. We must share our longhouse and build some new, smaller ones for our guests, even though some will want to build their own. Remember, the Iroquois have a tradition of being gracious and generous hosts."

In the crowd, Marty nudged Max. "What's a powwow?"

"It's a get-together of several tribes," Max whispered. "Sammy says it's a great celebration with feasts, singing and dancing, the smoking of peace pipes and other events, like lacrosse games and canoe races and storytelling."

"And a longhouse? It's what we're living in, right?"

"Ours is a miniature longhouse. They'll probably use it for storing things when we leave."

"I'm going to call it a shorthouse," Marty quipped.

Max ignored Marty's response.

"Sammy told me the Plains Indians—the buffalo hunters—lived in teepees. A teepee is made from a bunch of poles built into a cone, like an upside-down ice cream cone. You've seen them in Westerns, cowboy movies. The poles are covered with buffalo skins. Several people can live in a big one. There's a fire on the floor and the smoke rises out a hole in the roof."

"And a wigwam?"

"In the east, many Indian people lived in lodges or wigwams. The wigwam is made of bent saplings so it has a rounded top—like a tiny hockey rink. And it's covered by strips of bark sewn together."

"And we'll sleep on the hard ground?"

"No, of course not. We'll sleep on soft matting covered with deerskin."

Marty breathed a sigh of relief. "I think it's neat that you can have a fire right in the middle of your bedroom. If it's cold, the fire keeps you warm and you can even cook over it. But when I cook, I like to know there's a fire extinguisher handy."

"If you cook, there'll be enough smoke to drive all the mosquitoes away," Max said. "Anyway, we don't need a fire in our little house—not in the summer anyway."

"Okay, okay. One more question. Is the powwow open to the public? Mom and Dad and Uncle Jake might like to come. Dad could write a story about it for his newspaper."

"I'm sure Dad would like to write a story about it, and take photos too. But Sammy tells me this powwow won't be open to the public. We're welcome to stay though, as we're now honorary members of their community."

"I think I'll enter the dancing competition," Marty said, glancing at his brother, looking for a reaction.

"Oh, sure. You're a regular twinkletoes," Max said, laughing. "These will be serious tribal dances and you don't know any of them."

"I've got a week to learn a couple," Marty said. "I may surprise you. If I'm good, I may become a ballet dancer and move to Moscow when I'm older."

"Spare me," laughed Max. "You in the Moscow Ballet? You'd have to dance on your toes, Marty. Wearing tights and slippers."

"You laugh. But I may do it. And I bet I'd be the first man from the North Country to do it."

"Yes, you would. But if you want to be a hero in Moscow, go over there and teach them how to play hockey. They don't play the game and I bet they'd love it."

"I may just do that, too."

"Just be careful you don't get mixed up and wear your skates on the stage and your ballet slippers to a hockey game. By the way, there's no bodychecking in ballet."

"You mock me, Flying Hare. But I'll bet you a dollar I get a standing ovation when I dance during the powwow."

"You're on, Puny Turtle. It'll be the easiest dollar I ever earned."

"Again you mock me, using my Indian name in jest. But I'm not offended. I'm beginning to like that name and proud of it, in fact. Now leave me, Hairy Fly—I mean Flying Hare—I'm going to write a letter home telling Mom and Dad how brave I was yesterday and how you almost wet yourself when the big bad bear jumped up and frightened you half to death."

"You do that, and I'll write home and tell them the real truth," Max threatened. Laughing aloud, Max nudged Big Fella gently with his foot, then reached out and pulled his brother to his feet.

"Come on, you two, we're going to find Sammy."

They found their friend surrounded by a group of young children listening intently as Sammy entertained them with a story.

"Almost 250 years ago, we lost many of our best Iroquois warriors to war and disease. So we tried to rebuild our population by adopting people from other tribes. Sometimes we even adopted people from the white race—like my friends Max and Marty. Fellas, I'll bet you never heard the story of the capture of the little girl Eunice."

"No, we haven't," Max said. "My brother reads nothing but Hardy Boys books."

The children laughed. "Eunice. What a strange name," one of them said. "Was she pretty?"

"Please. No more interruptions," Sammy said, smiling. "I want this to be a short story. But yes, Eunice was very pretty. She had blond hair and sparkling blue eyes and she was only seven years old when our story takes place—in 1703.

"At that time, we had many battles with the white man and our population declined. So several of our tribes got together and went on the warpath, even though it was winter with much snow on the ground. Wearing snowshoes, our braves travelled over many mountains to a place in the east. They made a surprise attack on a village and captured over 100 residents."

"I'll bet Eunice was one of them," a small voice said.

Sammy frowned and raised a finger to his lips.

"Yes, Eunice was one of them," he continued. "And her father was the town's leading citizen, Reverend Williams. Our warriors herded all of the captives together and rushed them north along the frozen rivers. Those who could not keep up were left to perish on the ice. Our warriors were pursued by a huge force of military men with many guns but our men moved fast on their snowshoes, as fast as a flying hare."

Sammy paused to wink at Max.

"It took our warriors many days to reach the North Country, where they were treated as heroes. Little Eunice was the youngest of the captives, and the most popular. Reverend Williams, also a captive, even thanked our warriors for treating his daughter with so much tenderness.

"When our tribes returned to their villages, Eunice was adopted by one of the Indian families. She learned our Indian ways. She was loved and happy. In her former life, she had been disciplined by the end of a birch rod. When our people ransomed Reverend Williams back to his people, Eunice refused to leave with him. At age 15, she married a wise young brave who was also very handsome. For all but the first six years of her life, which stretched to 90 years, Eunice lived among us. By the way, Eunice had many children and one of her descendants lives with us in our village today. Can you guess who she is?"

"Tell us, Sammy. Tell us."

"She is our wonderful medicine woman, the widow Maude Greentree."

A hand flew up. "Then Mrs. Greentree's daughter, Susan, is related to Eunice as well."

Sammy laughed. "That's right. Susan Greentree is 16 now and one of the most popular young women in our village. Her family tree goes all the way back to Eunice. And even beyond. And that's my story for today."

The children applauded. One shouted, "Thank you, Sammy. You tell great stories."

Sammy laughed. "Thank you. Come back tomorrow if you want to hear another one. Now I must talk with Max and Marty. Like Eunice, perhaps they'll still be living with us when they are old and feeble."

"Yes! Yes!" shouted the children. "Stay with us, Max and Marty."

The Mitchell brothers laughed and waved to the children.

"Gosh, wouldn't that change our lives," Marty sighed. He thought of his room at home with hockey photos pinned to the walls, his mother's great cooking, his friends at school. "Forever? That's a long time. I'll have to think about it."

Max said, "Don't think, Marty. Do it! Look at this great village. There's hunting and fishing, lacrosse and canoeing. And the women do most of the work! You'd fit right in."

"Nope. Can't do it," Marty said. "My family, my friends, all the high school girls in Indian River—even my brother—would die of heartbreak if I stayed here."

Max threw up his arms. "I tried, Sammy," he said. "If Marty stayed, you could tell him all about your fascinating history."

"We are survivors," Sammy said with a smile. "And proud of it. We have survived five centuries of people from other lands coming here and pushing us around. At first we welcomed the foreigners. We fed them and traded with them. Then they began to steal our land. They killed us when we began to fight back. My ancestors say some early day explorers even put smallpox germs in our blankets to kill us off faster."

"They put germs in your blankets?" Marty said, shuddering. "That's disgusting."

Sammy nodded. "Some of the white people sought gold, others traded for our beaver skins. The French loved wearing those silly beaverskin hats. Some traded with us fairly, others tried to cheat us."

"A lot of what we know about Indian history has come from the movies," Max said solemnly.

"Oh, sure," Sammy said. "On the screen, you see the howling savages, the Indians attacking a train of covered wagons with their bows and arrows. The hero saying to the camera, 'The only good Indian is a dead Indian,' and everyone in the audience cheers when our people are slaughtered. You never hear or see what great riders our cousins, the Comanches, were. They could ride under the belly of a horse to avoid being shot. They could shoot their arrows with speed and deadly accuracy. But the movies show our people acting recklessly, falling off their horses and getting killed in great numbers. When the white man won a battle, it was called a great victory. When the Indians won, it was called a massacre. Our native actors should refuse to appear in those movies. Let those Hollywood people get Italian or Norwegian extras to play the Indian parts. That would be funny."

"Speaking of funny," Max said, "My brother Marty says he's going to learn an Indian dance and perform in the powwow. Would that embarrass you, Sammy?"

Sammy laughed. "Of course not. Powwows are mostly fun times. Everybody dances."

"Is there anything Marty and I can do to help?"

"Actually, there is. I know what a great hockey

player you are. And a fine baseball pitcher too. But have you ever played lacrosse?"

"I love lacrosse," Max said enthusiastically. "But I've never played in a league. Just pickup games. Why do you ask?"

"Because there will be a big lacrosse tournament during the powwow," Sammy said. "Five tribes competing. And our tribe is short of good players. Since you're an honorary member, I'm sure you qualify. Marty too, if he's a player."

"Marty's a goaltender in hockey—and a good one. But he's never played lacrosse."

"That's okay. I already have a goaltender in Elmo Swift. He's a hothead but he's quick. And he's been known to use his stick on a few opponents. So you're on my team. I'll get you a stick and equipment. We practice later today. But first, let's go tell the Great Chief and make sure you're eligible."

They reached the longhouse and Sammy knocked lightly on the door. He turned to the Mitchell brothers.

"Fellows, about what I said before. Can you blame our ancestors for fighting for their land—and their lives?"

"No, we can't, Sammy," Max said. "It's just that we've never heard your side of the story."

At that moment, the door swung open and Chief Echo ushered them in.

CHAPTER 5

MEETING SUSAN IN
THE LONGHOUSE

In the longhouse, Chief Echo said, "Of course Max is eligible to play lacrosse. It's a game of speed, stamina and strength, which he appears to have in abundance. The Iroquois invented lacrosse many moons ago. Sometimes villages played other villages, with up to 100 players on each team."

"Do you know why the game has a French name?" Max asked.

Chief Echo explained, "At first it was called 'galahs'—an Oneida name. Later, a French missionary saw us playing the game. He thought our lacrosse stick looked like a Bishop's crook or crosier—so he called it 'la crosse.' The name stuck."

The Chief noticed Max looking around the longhouse with great curiosity. "Have you ever seen a longhouse before, Max?"

"No, sir."

"Well, look around. Make yourself at home. A long-house is just that—a longhouse with a bark-covered curved roof. This longhouse is the cultural centre of our village. Several families, all related, live in a longhouse and here the woman is boss. If her daughter marries, the son-in-law moves in. We simply knock out one end of the house and add another room. In the old days, some longhouses were 400 feet long. This one's about 80 feet long."

"The woman is boss?" Max asked. "I thought you were the boss, Chief Echo."

"I am the Chief. The women of the tribe select the chief. Membership in a tribe passes through the female line. If a woman is an eagle clan member, her children will be eagle clan members. We even have a woman who is our village doctor: a medicine woman whose name is Maude Greentree. She knows some amazing cures, passed down to her over the generations." He winked at Max and added, "Yes, she makes house calls." The old Chief laughed heartily at his own joke and the young men laughed along with him.

They laughed even louder when Marty piped up, "I bet she makes longhouse calls, too. Especially since she lives in one."

Max walked up and down the longhouse, noting the various compartments, the rounded roof, the bark walls, the porches at each end holding corn and other food stored in bark containers. Cots for sleeping lined the walls with storage places built above them. There were several hearths for fires and some holes in the roof to let the smoke escape. In foul weather, the holes could easily be covered with large pieces of bark. There were woven mats on the floor. It was warm and rainproof and everyone he met was cheerful and friendly.

In one compartment he saw a young woman sitting on a mat in a corner. Her nimble fingers worked needle and thread through a pattern on a quilt. She looked up with a dazzling smile. Her skin was golden brown and her hair, lighter in colour than the rest of the women he'd seen, fell down her back in a long braid. "Hello, Mr. Max. My name is Susan Greentree."

"Pleased to meet you, Susan," said Max. "Sammy Fox was telling me your family story."

She smiled. "Sammy loves to tell tales, especially the one about Eunice." Susan put aside her quilt and rose awkwardly to her feet. She reached for a crutch that leaned against a wall.

"What happened?" asked Max.

"I twisted my ankle. I get around with my crutch, slowly but surely. My mother, the medicine woman, says I should be fine in a couple of days. See." Susan danced around in a little circle, mostly on one leg, the crutch supporting the other.

Max clapped his hands. "Well done, Susan."

Susan uttered a delightful laugh and said, "Welcome to our village, Max."

She shook him by the hand. He was embarrassed to discover he did not want to let go.

Max was about to speak when an old woman burst into the room. "I'm Esmerelda Echo, the Chief's wife." She pointed to the open door at the end of the longhouse. "When Echo is out there, wearing all his fancy feathers and looking so handsome, he's the big man. The one they all admire. The Grand Chief." She tapped a finger to her ample chest. "But inside this place, I'm the boss. You see good looking Indian girls in here, Max, and you want to talk with them, you ask me first. You got that?"

"Yes, ma'am," apologized Max hastily. She was squinting darkly, but Max noticed the trace of a smile on her lips. She escorted Max across the room, and then leaned into him conspiratorially.

"You seen any yet?" Esmerelda asked. "Any good lookers?"

"Well, yes," Max answered. "I've seen one." His glance traveled across the room to where Susan had taken up her quilt.

The old woman nodded. She whispered, "Susan, she's a prize. Someday she'll move away from the reserve and go to college. She'll be a great doctor like her mother—only learn different methods and new treatments from white teachers. Not better methods, just different."

Changing the subject, she raised a fat finger at him and said in mock anger, "And don't get my floor dirty, Blondie. If you do, you'll have to sweep it."

"Yes, ma'am. I wiped my feet on the mat before I came in."

Sammy Fox sauntered up, laughing. "Blondie? Is that your new nickname, Max?"

"Don't you dare stick that name on me," Max growled. "If you do, you'll have to find another hockey team to play on next season."

Later, Chief Echo invited Max, Marty and Sammy into his compartment. It was separated from the rest of the longhouse by a wicker screen. The young men sat cross-legged on the floor, sharing a colourful woven mat.

"Boys—men, I should say—I have a problem that I want to share with you," the Chief began. "Sammy, you know our reserve is not large. To the north, where the road enters our land, there is a tract of land—about 500 acres—that lies between the reserve and the mining town of Silver Creek."

"Silver Creek is a tough community, like a lot of mining towns," Sammy explained to Max. "You and Marty were there. Imagine charging a quarter to use the men's room! That bully you met was Blackjack Bradley. He's got two sons, Bart and Hugo. They're just as mean-tempered as their dad. Soon there won't be any silver left to mine. The miners the Bradleys hire—most of them—are a bunch of thugs. We drive all the way to Indian River if we need supplies. Going into Silver City is too dangerous. At least it is for native people. They don't want us around there."

The Chief raised his hand and Sammy stopped talking.

"The land I refer to is not very fertile," said the Chief. "It is rocky, as you know. Fortunately, there is a small lake on it, with beautiful clear water in which many fish can be caught. It's also a place where game can be hunted when they come to drink. Our people go there often.

"A few days ago, I heard strange sounds coming from that vacant land so I went to investigate. I was surprised to find a crew of men chopping down trees for lumber or firewood and taking rock samples. I suppose they were looking for veins of silver. I ordered them to leave at once."

"And what happened, Chief? Did they leave?"

He shook his head. "They said they were working for Blackjack Bradley and they had no intention of leaving. They told me to get out of their way and mind my own business." Chief Echo's lined face grew taut with hot anger. "They called me a 'stupid old redskin.' They said they could do whatever they liked on that parcel of land because Blackjack owned it."

"And what did you say, Chief? What did you do?"

The Chief sighed, composing himself. "Normally, I would follow an old Indian proverb: 'Do not judge your neighbour until you walk two moons in his moccasins.' But in this case, walking in the Bradley moccasins would only make my feet feel dirty. So I pulled this piece of paper from my pocket." He held a faded document up to the light. "I told them it was a deed, that the land belonged to the Iroquois.

"One of them—it was Bart Bradley—came over and grabbed the paper. He pushed me to the ground and kicked me in the leg. He looked at the paper, spit on it and threw it in my face. He said it meant nothing. Indians had no money to buy land. They left me there and went back to work. So I came home. Bart's brother Hugo followed me for a time, calling me names, but always keeping well back."

"It is easy to be brave from a distance," Max said, remembering a phrase his father had once said.

The old Chief lifted his robe to examine a deep bruise on his leg.

Max was shocked. "Shouldn't you go to town and see a doctor?"

"Bah!" scowled the Chief. "The medicine woman will treat my leg. Make it well in a couple of days. She's smarter than any town doctor."

"Chief Echo," Sammy interrupted politely.

"Wasn't Bart right, or partially right? Isn't it true that Indians don't own land? We were given land by the government to live on."

The Chief frowned thoughtfully. "For most tribes, the land that was left over when the whites divided up the country was given to the Indians—even though we were here first. Government leaders bragged, 'Look how generous we are. We have given you all these little bits of land.' It was never the best land and I guess they forgot it was ours to begin with.

"Now let me tell you more about the vacant land next to our reserve. Many years ago, a young Iroquois went to the government and said, 'We want that 500 acres of useless land to hunt and fish on.'

"The government men laughed and said, 'No, you have enough land. Besides, that land you speak of has no value. It was burned out by a fire.'

"The young Iroquois said, 'If you won't give me that land, let me buy it from you for 500 dollars.'

"The government man said, 'Now you're talking.' He took the money and gave the young Iroquois a piece of paper, stating he owned that useless land.

"The Iroquois used all his savings, plus some money handed down from his father and his grandfather to buy the 500 acres north of our reserve.

"It was true that all the trees had burned down. Now, the trees are back and the land has repaired itself. Now, what seemed worthless land years ago may be very valuable. And that wise Iroquois still owns the land he bought, no matter what Bradley claims."

"Who was that wise Iroquois, Great Chief?" Sammy asked. "Do I know him?"

"You do indeed." He smiled and pointed to a signature on the paper. "That is my name on this deed."

CHAPTER 6

DEALING WITH DYNAMITE

The DeSoto was ten years old. Pockmarked with rust holes and sporting a rumble seat in back, it bucked and snorted as it rolled along the unpaved road leading to Indian River. Sammy Fox was driving and Max sat next to him. In the pop-open rumble seat, Chief Echo sat stoically next to Marty, the wind whistling in their ears. Big Fella had been left back at the village because the children on the reserve had become fond of him.

"We have only four cars and a truck on our reserve, but this is the best vehicle by far," Sammy was saying. "We use the truck when we go into town for supplies. It's less likely to get swallowed up by a pothole and come out somewhere in China."

"Wasn't DeSoto a Spanish explorer who visited North America after Columbus?" Max asked Sammy, pointing at the name on the dashboard.

"Yes, he was, but like Columbus, he was no friend

to our people. I wouldn't name a car after that ras-
cal. One of our elders was given this car by a rela-
tive. He was so ashamed to drive it he painted over
the name DeSoto everywhere it appeared. But he
forgot the dash. I told him to paint a sign on the
back. 'This car is not a DeSoto—it's a Disaster.' But
he didn't do it. DeSoto came to the southeastern
part of the United States in 1539, but not to the
North Country, thank goodness. He came with 600
warriors and many guns. Our cousins in the south
hated him because he stole their corn, kidnapped
their men and women and caused death and
destruction. Our people seethed with anger. Later,
at a place called Mabila, our cousins ambushed him
and killed many of his soldiers. But the diseases he
and his men brought wiped out thousands of
natives. The good news is he never found the gold
he sought. And he too died of a deadly disease. I say
good riddance to him."

Sammy slapped the steering wheel of the car as if
he were slapping the late explorer on the cheek.

"One of our tribes chased the rest of his men
down the Mississippi River. The Spaniards sailed
away in their big ships while our people shouted,
'You are the savages, not us. If we had bigger canoes,
we would chase you across the sea and conquer you
and show you no mercy.'"

"I didn't know that about DeSoto," Max said

thoughtfully. "I always thought the early explorers were brave men, heroic people who helped establish a great nation."

"Bah!" snorted Sammy. "Maybe heroes to some," he said bitterly. "To us they were greedy, ruthless men who cared nothing for the Indian culture. They were looking for gold and slaves and furs. And land—always more land. And they were arrogant. They thought their ways were the best ways—the only ways. But Max, I'm talking too much. We're almost there, aren't we?"

"Around the next bend in the road, my friend."

On the street outside the grocery store, Harry and Amy Mitchell were waiting in the family car for their sons to show up. Following a joyful reunion, and an introduction to Chief Echo, they went into the store and ordered ice cream cones.

"You boys look good," said Amy Mitchell to her sons. "Life at Tumbling Waters really agrees with you. But my goodness, what happened to your hair?"

Max and Marty told their folks all about the game they'd played and how they'd been captured and how they'd been "scalped."

"What's the loss of a little hair?" Marty interjected, wiping ice cream from his chin. "If the gods make me rich."

"Max," asked Harry Mitchell, "You said you had something urgent to tell us. What's up?"

"Dad, Chief Echo has a big problem. You might be able to help him. Maybe through the power of the press. Or maybe you've got a lawyer friend..."

Chief Echo picked up the story, adding more details. He told Harry Mitchell how he'd encountered the Bradley gang on land that he owned. And how badly he'd been treated. The Chief unfolded the old deed to the land and showed it to Harry.

"Looks legit to me," said Mr. Mitchell. "The signature is a bit blurred."

"That's where Bart Bradley spit on it," the Chief explained. "But I assure you, it is my signature."

"Why'd he spit on it?"

"Bart Bradley threw the deed in the Chief's face—after kicking him," Sammy said. "Bart said the deed wasn't worth spit. Then he spat on the Chief's signature."

"We don't need a problem like this right now," the Chief said quietly. "Many people are coming for our big powwow next week and they have to use the road through that land to get to our village. I'm worried Bradley and his gang will make trouble. The Bradleys have guns. Someone may get hurt."

"Let me take a few notes," Harry Mitchell said, pulling a notepad from his pocket.

"I took the deed to the sheriff in Silver City," Chief Echo said. "He said the deed probably wasn't legal."

"Did he say why?" asked Mitchell.

"He told me he didn't trust... Indians." The Chief shook his head. "Then he told me to get out of his office. I found out later that he was Blackjack Bradley's first cousin. They call him Banjo Billy Bradley."

Harry Mitchell scribbled furiously. "Well," he said, pausing, "a sheriff isn't likely to know about such things, especially if he's a Bradley. A smart lawyer would know."

"Mr. Mitchell, we can't afford a lawyer. Twenty-five dollars is a lot of money to us."

"I understand, sir. Listen, Amy and I will talk about the situation on the way back to Indian River. Maybe there's something we can do. Sounds like it might be a story for my newspaper. A story Max can help research, since he's at the scene. Max is a good reporter. He knows the importance of getting all the facts."

"You boys be careful with Blackjack Bradley," cautioned Amy Mitchell. "He's notorious throughout the North Country."

"We will, Mom," promised Max and Marty.

There was more small talk, and then Harry Mitchell looked at his watch. "Got to go, men," he said. "Got a paper to get out. We'll talk again soon."

On the way back to the reserve, Sammy told Max to look in the glove compartment of the car. "There's a copy of a letter in there, written by one of my heroes, Chief Seattle, to the President of the United States sometime in the 1800s. He wrote it after the U.S. government pressured him to sell his land. I must have read it a thousand times. It proves that a Native American can be as eloquent as any man can. Read it, Max. As a writer, you're going to love Chief Seattle's words. Somebody must have appreciated him, because they named a city after him."

Max found the letter, unfolded it, and began to read. His words were articulate and touching. Chief Seattle wrote about mankind's connectedness to the earth, and argued that one cannot "buy" land because it is a part of everyone. Furthermore, Chief Seattle urged the President of the United States to remember that, if his tribe does sell the government any land, that land is sacred—because air, water, and the earth's creatures are precious to all humans. The Chief also asserted that all men, regardless of the colour of their skin, are brothers on this earth.

"Wow!" Max uttered. "It really makes you think."

Sammy smiled. He was delighted that Chief Seattle's letter had struck a chord in Max.

Over the roar of the noisy engine, Max heard an explosion like thunder.

"Listen! Sammy, did you hear a funny sound—like a boom?"

"Yes, I did," Sammy said, slowing down. "There's another one—and a third. Boom! Boom! Boom!

What could it be? It's not thunder, is it?"

"Couldn't be. The sky is perfectly clear."

"We heard it, too," Marty shouted from the rumble seat.

"Let's try to find out what it is," Sammy said, changing gears and speeding up. In minutes, he turned the old DeSoto into the road leading to the reserve. But when he swept between a row of trees, he slammed on the brakes and the car began to skid on the soft ground.

"Hold tight!" he shouted. He jerked the steering wheel to avoid a huge hole in the road. The car skidded and almost flipped over. It crashed hard into some bushes. Everyone was thrown forward but fortunately no one was injured.

They leaped out of the car and examined the deep hole.

"Wow!" cried Marty. "If we'd driven in there, we'd have been killed. Looks like a meteorite from outer space landed here."

"It wasn't a meteorite," remarked Chief Echo grimly.

"Then what caused it, sir?"

"Dynamite."

"Dynamite?" chorused the Mitchell brothers.

"Wait a minute, fellows." Sammy said. "We heard two or three more booms, didn't we? Where do you suppose they came from?"

"Sammy, get in the car. See if you can back it up," directed the Chief. "We'll drive along the tree line. There must be an old logging trail we can use to get back into the village."

They jumped back into the car and Sammy backed up. Then he drove carefully over the rocky terrain. Just as he passed the beautiful blue lake, he saw something out of the corner of his eye.

"Oh, no!" he exclaimed.

"What is it, Sammy?" Max asked.

"Look! On the lake! Dozens of dead fish. Hundreds of them. Somebody exploded dynamite in the water."

"It must have been the Bradleys and their thugs," said Chief Echo. "They're out to frighten us, to show us who's boss. See! They even left a sign by the lake. It says: Indians keep out! No fishin'. This meens you!"

"Gee, they can't even spell," muttered Marty. "What'll we do now, Chief?"

"Look! There's the logging trail through the woods, one used by the horses. It'll be narrow but usable. When we get back to the village we'll plan our next move."

Back on the reserve, Max, Marty and Sammy were allowed to stay and listen when Chief Echo gathered his elders together in the longhouse. Chief Echo handed out cups of steaming tea and sweet rolls his wife Esmerelda had prepared. From behind the Chief's back, she winked at Max, and then pointed at his feet. "No dirt," she mouthed silently. He smiled and mouthed back, "Clean. Very clean moccasins."

"It saddens me that we cannot find a way to live in harmony with our neighbours," the Chief said, a frown creasing his forehead. "We have no quarrel with Bradley and the miners in Silver City. My father often said, 'The greatest strength is gentleness.' But we must not let them take what is not theirs. We must face up to them. We must have a plan. And we must prepare wisely and quickly, because tomorrow our visitors will start arriving for the big powwow."

CHAPTER 7
THE POWWOW BEGINS

When the boys left the Chief's longhouse an hour later, a plan had been concocted. It was agreed that several young villagers would slip through the woods to the north and make their way to the main road. There, some distance north of the mining town of Silver City, they would wait for the various tribes coming from that direction. Most would be in automobiles. The Iroquois youths would guide the visitors through old logging trails, like the one they had driven over that afternoon, in a roundabout route to the reserve, bypassing the roughnecks in the mining town. A similar number of villagers would meet tribes approaching from the south and guide them to the village, also leading them to the site through the "back door." Other young men from the reserve, wielding axes, saws and hatchets, would clear the routes of undergrowth to provide easy access.

Because the main road passing through Silver City

was seldom used, chances were good that no traffic would see the convoy of cars carrying tribe members to the powwow, as they left the main road and disappeared into the woods. With a little deception and a little luck, the miners in Silver City would never know about the powwow. If the miners had heard about the powwow but no Indians from other places travelled along their main street, they would assume that Blackjack Bradley had frightened Chief Echo so badly that he had cancelled any plans for a tribal reunion.

The plan worked to perfection.

The village of Tumbling Waters soon quadrupled in size as families large and small arrived for the great celebration. Vehicles appeared to sigh in relief after traversing the bumpiest trails they'd ever encountered. One ancient Ford was the last to arrive. Steam seeped from its radiator as it rolled awkwardly along on two flat tires. Everyone cheered the intrepid driver when he leaped from the vintage vehicle and kissed the ground. He would have kissed the hood of the Ford but he was afraid of burning his mouth on the hot metal.

After embracing old friends and exchanging small gifts—handsome deerskin pouches adorned with porcupine quills, miniature wooden war canoes, stuffed dolls and combs decorated with carved animal figures—the guests gathered near the blazing fire where Chief Echo, dressed in his ceremonial robes, delivered a message of welcome. Then the women of the reserve, smiling broadly, mingled with their guests, serving hot tea and warm biscuits smothered with sweet strawberry jam, whetting the visitors' appetites for a delectable brunch to follow. The families then set to work, skillfully erecting temporary living quarters that popped up everywhere. They lit fires, stowed their belongings and went to bathe in the nearby river. Small children went wading and swimming, others went exploring, climbing rock formations and running through open fields. Still others challenged cousins to canoe races, games of hopscotch and target-shooting contests using small bows and arrows. The older boys tossed lacrosse balls around, warming up for the tournament that would take place later that afternoon.

Many of the teenagers looked at Max and Marty with great curiosity, obviously wondering why two outsiders were attending a powwow. But they showed good manners. They said nothing and asked no questions. And when Max and Marty grabbed lacrosse sticks and joined in the fun, the young visitors nodded approvingly at the skills they displayed at passing and catching the ball.

Then a caller, a young Iroquois shouting "Hi, yi, yi, yi!" summoned everyone to a central meeting place for a procession to mark the official opening of the powwow. Select members of the various tribes, led by the elders who were dressed in colourful Indian regalia, including huge feathered headdresses, shawls and jackets adorned with bright multi-coloured beads and necklaces, marched in a circle to the beat of a drum. This was followed by a flag rais-ing ceremony and short speeches by tribal leaders in a language Max and Marty could not understand.

"They are stressing the need for solidarity between our tribes," Sammy explained. "They say it is vital to hand down our traditions from generation to gener-ation. There will be more ceremonial dances later."

At the brunch, guests feasted on delicacies like venison, roast duck, fish, corn bread, wild berries and hot tea.

After everyone had had their fill, the Great Chief entertained them with the first of what would be many tales this celebration week. The guests fell into respectful silence.

"Let me tell you the story of Samoset and Squanto," he began. "When the Pilgrims landed at Plymouth Rock on March 16, 1621, our cousin, Samoset, walked out of the forest and waved to them. Speaking words he had learned from traders who had preceded the Pilgrims, Samoset soon had the newcomers smiling and waving back when he shouted, 'Welcome, Englishmen!'

"Those words broke any tension that existed

between our people and the English. Then another of our ancestors named Squanto, who spoke many languages, helped work out a treaty with the Pilgrims, one that brought four decades of peace between the immigrants and our people. Squanto moved in with the Pilgrims and taught them how to survive in a new and bewildering land. He showed them how to find food in the forest, how to catch tasty fish in a weir and how to use less-tasty fish as fertilizer between rows of corn he showed them how to plant. Thanks to Squanto, the Pilgrims were able to survive. Without him, they might have perished."

"It might have been better had the English died of starvation," a gruff voice said from the crowd. "Or frozen to death. They brought nothing but trouble. Didn't they wipe out Squanto's tribe?"

"Not deliberately," replied Chief Echo. "They took Squanto to England for a few weeks and when he returned he discovered all of his friends and family had been wiped out by an epidemic. The Pilgrims were very sympathetic to the plight of Squanto's people.

"Most of the Englishmen showed greater immunity to their own diseases and survived. Our ancestors had never encountered such diseases. They died in great numbers and the few who lived were very bitter and angry with the Europeans. My friend, there are many who would agree with you, about the English, the French, the Spanish—all the people who came to our shores. War and disease decimated our tribes. Our culture was all but destroyed. History has not been kind to the North American Indian. But what is past and cannot be prevented, should not be grieved for. We should pursue wisdom, not knowledge. Knowledge is of the past, wisdom is of the future."

Chief Echo held up his right hand to silence the discontented murmurings.

"My friends and brothers," he intoned deeply. "This week we pause to celebrate the goodness that exists in all of us, the friendship we feel for each other, the forgiveness we feel for those who invaded us. But we must not blame their descendants. In fact, there are two in our midst—two fine young men to whom we open our arms in welcome. I refer to Flying Hare and Puny Turtle—Max and Marty Mitchell."

There was a smattering of applause. People turned to stare at the Mitchell brothers and most of the faces bore smiles.

The old Chief then announced the winner of a special Award of Honour, given to a community member or members for distinguished service.

"Last year," he said, "we recognized several of our Mohawk brothers who helped build the Empire State Building in New York City. Brave workers who confronted terrifying dangers fearlessly. Many of our young men excel at working on thin steel beams at incredible heights—and they do it while laughing at the risks.

"This year, we salute a young man who has proved himself worthy on the athletic field. This fine athlete has not only displayed exceptional ability in sports, excelling at hockey and lacrosse, but he is a valued member of our community, always willing to assist the old and teach the young. For his storytelling qualities alone, he would be a worthy candidate for this award. His reward is a splendid trophy as well as a valuable quilt with patches telling the history of our tribe. The winner is Sammy Running Fox."

The crowd burst into wild applause. Max and Marty may have been clapping the loudest. They were thrilled that their close friend had been recognized in this way.

Max noticed that Elmo Swift, sitting off to the side, jumped to his feet, and with a disgusted look at Sammy, stormed off. "I guess he thinks he should have won," Max said to Marty.

Marty thumbed his nose at Elmo's back. "Let him go," he said scornfully. "No one likes a sore loser."

Max raised a finger to his lips. "Chief Echo is about to speak again."

"One of the most popular events at a powwow,

and one of the most competitive, is the lacrosse tournament," the Chief stated. "Today, the first games in the tournament will be played."

A loud cheer erupted from the crowd.

The Chief smiled broadly. "But before we move to the lacrosse field, the young men and women of our tribe will entertain you with an ancient inter-tribal dance."

He sat down and the beat of the drums began. Young girls and boys who'd been 'waiting in the wings'—which, in this case, meant behind a large bush—came dancing into view to much applause. Their beaming faces, colourful costumes and dancing feet brought joy to the event and they were wildly applauded when they finished their dance.

Suddenly, to everyone's surprise, a dancing bear flew from behind the bush. The bear snorted and growled and rolled on the ground. It gained its feet and did a somersault, then another. It stood upright and twirled several times until it staggered drunkenly and fell down, dizzy from the effort. Everyone began to laugh at the antics of the dancing bear. On all fours, the bear waddled over to one of the young female dancers, rose on its hind legs and attempted to waltz with her. But she was not familiar with the movements and stepped on the bear's foot. He feigned injury and fell down, howling in pain, then limped away, pausing before he hid behind the bush to wave both paws at the spectators. His act was hilarious.

The people rose and applauded.

"Can you guess who was inside that costume?" Sammy asked.

"No need to guess. It was that silly brother of mine," Max sighed. "He bet me a dollar he'd get a standing ovation at the powwow by dancing. But I never thought he'd do it as a bear."

Sammy chortled. "You might say he... bearly won the bet!"

Max laughed too. "That brother of mine always has something, ahem, brewing."

CHAPTER 8

THE LACROSSE TOURNAMENT

Clad in lacrosse gear, Max took his position at forward as a member of the Tumbling Waters team, the Porcupines, led by Sammy Fox. "I chose the name because porcupines are great at defense," Sammy said. "We will be, too. Skunks may be better defensive animals, but who wants to be known as a skunk?" Max knew only two of his teammates by name— Sammy, who played centre, and goalie Elmo Swift.

"Elmo's nickname is 'Smiley,'" Sammy had whispered to Max in the warm-up. "Because he's such a sourpuss. Nobody ever calls him that to his face for fear of backlash. Just be careful around him."

"Good thing we're on the same team," Max replied with a grin. "Know what? I'm going to call him 'Swifty.' He should like that."

Sammy laughed as he took his place for the opening draw against the Kickapoos. The ball was faced off and the game began.

The field of play was ringed with dozens of enthu-siastic fans. They cheered wildly for their favourite team. The play was extremely fast and aggressive, marked by clashing sticks and the crunch of body contact. The goalies were lightly padded, wearing old hockey goal pads, a chest protector, hockey pants, elbow pads and gloves. Max marveled at how quickly the ball moved from stick to stick. Every player was so clever at trapping the ball in the leather webbing or pocket at the end of his stick and releasing a pass or a shot on goal with lightning-quick speed.

"I'll have to be at my very best to keep up with these fellows," Max told Marty. "I know I can run with them. It's just that I've never played at such a high level."

"Don't worry about it. You'll show them," Marty answered.

The contest was a thriller. Sammy Fox scored the first two goals, but the Kickapoos stormed back to tie the score. Just before halftime, Sammy fed Max a quick pass and the field was partially open ahead of him.

"Go, Max!" shouted Sammy.

Max took off, twisting to dodge one check, turn-ing to avoid another, and then he was in the clear. He raced in on the goalie, faked a shot to one corner, faked again to the other corner and gracefully flicked the ball through the goalie's legs. Goal!

As the crowd roared, the goalie slammed his stick on the net, angry with himself for being so easily duped. He glared at Max and snarled, "You were lucky." When Max brushed by him, the goalie stuck the knob of his stick in Max's ribs, knocking the breath out of him. Max was tempted to retaliate, then thought better of it. "I'll be back," he gasped. "You'd better be ready."

At halftime, the Porcupines led by one goal.

In the second half, both Max and Sammy were covered aggressively. When either player carried the ball up the field, his opponents harassed him. The two Porcupine stars were elbowed and high-sticked and fouled while the referee, who happened to be the uncle of the opposing team's goalie, looked the other way.

Late in the game, a Kickapoo forward raced in and laced a shot at Elmo Swift. "Nice stop, Swifty!" Max called out in praise as the ball bounced off Elmo's stick and rolled to the side. Elmo darted out of his net after the bouncing ball just as Max, who was checking back, went to retrieve it. "I've got it, Elmo," Max shouted a warning as he snagged the ball in the webbing of his stick. But Elmo didn't hear or wasn't listening. Running hard but off balance, the goalie ran into Max headfirst, knocking him to the grass. Elmo tumbled down on top of him.

The ball squirted away, right into the path of an opposing player. He snagged it, whirled and fired the ball into the Porcupine's empty net. The Kickapoos rejoiced. Tie score!

"Dern it," Elmo shrieked, giving Max a hard shove in the ribs as he got to his feet. "Look what you've gone and done. They've tied the score and it's all you're fault."

"Take it easy, Elmo," Max said calmly as his teammates gathered around. "I told you I had the loose ball. Guess you didn't hear me. It was just an accident. Nobody's fault."

"Accident!" cried Elmo. "I say you deliberately ran into me. Made me look like a fool. Why don't you go back where you belong? You're not one of us. Go back to Indian River!"

"Listen, Elmo. I was invited here so this is where I belong. Be reasonable. It's just a game we're playing. We can beat these guys. Just calm down."

But Elmo wasn't listening. Angrily, he threw off his goal pads, yanked off his jersey and belly pad and tossed his gloves aside.

"I won't take orders from an outsider," he shouted. He slammed his stick to the ground. He picked it up again and brandished it at Max. "I should belt you with this," he threatened. Instead, he lifted some grassy turf out of the webbing and threw it in Max's face.

Max raised his fists, then caught himself and pulled back. He was a guest and realized he had to control himself. He felt a tug on his elbow. Marty was gripping his jersey, easing him away from the furious goaltender.

"Easy does it, brother," said Marty, "Don't let him provoke you into a fight."

"You're right, Marty, besides, fighting with Smiley... I mean Elmo... isn't worth it," chuckled Max.

"Smiley! You call me Smiley? Nobody calls me that," Elmo shrieked.

Enraged, he lunged at Max, arms extended, charging like a stampeding bull. Max nimbly stepped aside at the last second, like a Spanish bullfighter.

Elmo lunged past him, snorting furiously. He spun around and lunged again. This time, Max slipped both arms around Elmo's waist, hoisted him high in the air with surprising agility and strength, spun him around, then slammed him to the hard ground where he landed on his back. All the wind was knocked out of the goaltender.

"Oooph!" he moaned. Elmo lay there, stunned and gasping for air.

He staggered to his feet, holding one hand to his ribs. Avoiding Max, he limped gingerly toward the sidelines.

"Not going to play anymore, Smiley?" taunted Max.

Elmo's face turned beet red. He swung around and

glared at Max. "I'm through with lacrosse," he croaked. "But I'm not through with you."

A discontented murmur swept through the stunned crowd. Oldtimers had never seen two teammates involved in an altercation on the lacrosse field.

"It wasn't the white boy's fault," someone shouted. "That Swift kid always did have a rotten temper. The ref should have thrown him out of the game."

"It was a dern good game until Elmo lost his head," someone else observed loudly. "That kid needs to learn some restraint."

Just then, the referee pushed his way through the crowd. "Sorry, boys," he explained. "I was caught up the field. Lost one of my moccasins. Didn't see a thing..." The players and spectators rolled their eyes.

"Lost a moccasin, did you, ref?" one of the fans called out. "Did yer seein' eye dog find it for you?"

The fans laughed and the referee ignored the jibe. Or pretended to.

"There are still two minutes to play," the referee announced. "And overtime if the score is tied. Let's play."

"Sure, ref," Sammy Fox said. "But we've just lost our only goalie."

"Then play with your net empty," the ref suggested. He shrugged and walked away, putting some distance between himself and the fans.

"I've got a better idea," Max interjected. "Marty, you throw on those goal pads Elmo left behind."

"Me?" Marty exclaimed. "I've never played lacrosse in my life, Max. Not a real game, that is. You *know* that."

"You've played goal in hockey, haven't you? And played well, too. Now get that gear on. You'll find it's a fun game. It really is."

The crowd, intrigued by this development, stayed put. They wanted to see how this game would play out. The score was tied, the best goalie on the reserve had quit in a rage and now a newcomer to the village who'd never played lacrosse before was strapping on the pads.

After a few warm-up shots at Marty, half of which found their way into his net, prompting several of the onlookers to snicker and the Kickapoos to smile, the final minutes of the game were played.

The Porcupines gave their new goalie plenty of protection, allowing just one shot on goal, which Marty blocked awkwardly. Regulation time ended with the score tied at three.

There was a two-minute timeout before the sudden death overtime period. Players from both teams sprawled on the grass, sipping water from a wooden bucket and conserving their energy.

"Max, I know I look awkward, but I'm getting the hang of it," Marty said to Max before the overtime period began. "I'm used to moving on ice, not grass."

"It's just a game, Marty, win or lose," Max said.

The referee called for play to resume and the overtime minutes flew by. Both teams had good scoring chances, but both goalies excelled. Marty made several outstanding saves, one time sticking his neck in front of a shot. "Ouch!" he shouted. "That one hurt." Then he laughed and the crowd laughed with him.

With 15 seconds to play, Marty stopped a final hard shot and shovelled the ball to Max. "Looks like the game will end in a tie, Max," he shouted. "Time's almost up."

But Max was off and running with the ball. Fifteen seconds was plenty of time for a sprint down the field. He barrelled past one checker, then another. Out of the corner of his eye, off to his left, he saw Sammy racing to catch up. At midfield, Max faked a long shot on goal and two opposing players threw their sticks high in the air to block it. But Max wasn't shooting. He was passing. The ball flew right to Sammy's stick and lodged snugly in the webbing. Sammy didn't have to break stride. He raced in from the wing, warding off a check with one strong arm. With the other, he shot low to the goalie's stick side. The goalie kicked a leg out, then sprawled, grunting in frustration and disgust. He turned to see the goal judge raising a red flag and waving it in the air. Goal!

Max and his teammates mobbed Sammy. The Porcupines had won the first game of the tournament with two seconds to play—and with a pair of first-time players in the lineup. Both had played starring roles. The crowd surged onto the field. Marty raced along the grass to the far end of the field to join his mates, his leg pads flapping. He was whooping and hollering. The Porcupines turned to hug him and lifted him high in the air.

Max and Marty, with Sammy between them, three happy victors with their arms around each other's shoulders, left the field together. When they caught up to a young woman hobbling along with the help of a crutch, Sammy intercepted her and she gave him a hug. She looked shyly at Max and Marty, and then motioned them over. Smiling broadly, she hugged them too.

"Wow!" said Marty later. "Did you see how she hugged me? I think she really likes me. Being a lacrosse star has its advantages, doesn't it? Who is she, Sammy?"

Sammy smiled at Max, and then said, "Gee, I dunno, Marty. Never saw her before in my life."

"Oh, sure," muttered Marty, as the other two chuckled.

Max had been a competitor in many games—football, baseball and hockey. And he'd enjoyed his share of thrills and triumphs. But here, on this secluded patch of ground in Tumbling Waters, playing a game he'd known only a little, he'd just experienced one of his most satisfying moments in sports.

"Lacrosse is a great game," he said.

"And you're a great player," Sammy said. He laughed and added, "You wound up with two out of three goalies wanting to kill you."

"I tried to shake hands with the opposing goalie after the game, but he turned away. What a poor sport," Max said with a shrug. "Hey, guys," he said. "Do you think any World Series winner, or any Stanley Cup champion, ever felt any better than we do at this moment?"

"Heck, no." said Sammy, slapping Max on the back.

"They'd feel richer, maybe." Marty added. "But no better."

CHAPTER 9
TWO TOUGH COMPETITIONS

"Shooting arrows from a bow is an ancient skill," Sammy was saying. "The object is to guide the arrow through the air to the target, whether it be a deer or a bull's eye. Our people have always excelled as archers."

"Always?" asked Marty. "You mean like, for hundreds of years?"

"More like thousands," Sammy said. "And not only among our people. The elders told me that archery was big in Egypt over 5,000 years ago."

"We tried shooting arrows from a bow when we were younger," Max replied. "We pretended we were Robin Hood. Dad taught us how to shoot with a bow he used."

"Yeah, and we were pretty good, too," Marty added. "Well, Max was good. He wanted to try and shoot an apple off my head like William Tell, but I didn't think it was such a good idea."

"Neither did Mom and Dad," Max said, chuckling.

Marty said, "I was kinda wild with my shots. One day, I shot an arrow right through Mrs. Anderson's pink underpants, hanging on her clothesline. She's our neighbour. It was pretty funny."

"Mrs. Anderson didn't think so," Max said. "Mom made you go and apologize."

"Yeah, I offered to patch them up with hockey tape but she said forget about it. She said she should make me wear those underpants to school—over my school pants. But I talked her out of it."

Sammy smiled. "Too bad you won't be shooting at pink underpants today. You might win. But you'll see some fine shooting. We'll all be competing for a prize, though I admit Elmo Swift has the best chance of winning. He practices all the time. It would be great if one of us can beat him."

"I'll try to," Marty said, "Don't blame me if I hit somebody in the keister."

"How's the competition work, Sammy?" Max asked, ignoring his brother.

"We all take turns shooting at a deerskin target. The target is an outline of a bear with a red heart in the middle. Three shots per shooter. The shooter gets a point if he hits the bear and three points if he hits the heart. Most points wins. Come on, the competition is about to start. We'll share my bows and arrows."

Twenty or more shooters, young and old, lined up behind a chalk mark drawn across the grass. Fifty feet away was the bear-like target, stretched across some bales of straw. Ten shooters took aim and fired. Only two struck the bear—the others buried themselves in the straw.

Then it was Elmo Swift's turn. He took careful aim, steadied his bow and fired an arrow into the heart of the bear. "Oooh," said the onlookers. "Great shot, Elmo!"

Several more arrows thunked into the target, but none landed in the centre. Sammy came close. His arrow hit within an inch of the heart. Max was next. But when he drew back Sammy's bow, he found his hands were trembling. This is more difficult than I thought, he said to himself. He took a deep breath, steadied his hands and fired. The arrow flew straight at the heart but dipped slightly at the end of its flight and split the black line that outlined the heart.

A referee, a former expert archer named Stan Shoot From Horse, hurried over to examine the target. He came back to Max and said, "I'll give you that. Three points."

Elmo Swift exploded in anger. "You can't give him that shot," he yelped. "It wasn't fully in the heart."

"Stop whining, Elmo. On the line counts. That's how you won last year, remember?"

Marty was the last to shoot. He was so nervous he

had trouble inserting the arrow in the bowstring. It fell to the ground.

A smooth hand plucked it from the grass.

"Want some help, Marty?"

He turned and looked into the smiling face of Susan Greentree. He was speechless.

Susan laughed and said, "Hold my crutch. I'll notch this arrow for you."

Marty said, "Why don't you shoot it for me? I'm no good at this bow and arrow stuff, anyway."

Susan smiled and said, "Okay. Here's how we do it." She took a comfortable stance, raised the bow, carefully fitted the arrow, drew and released. Plunk! The arrow split the red heart of the bear.

"Wow!" Marty exclaimed.

"Holy smoke!" echoed Max.

A roar went up from the crowd. There was wild applause. Nobody had expected a young girl to shoot like a veteran. Susan, her face flushed, turned and nodded to the spectators. "Thank you."

"Next round," declared the referee.

A breeze swept across the range and the shooters had even more difficulty hitting the target. Elmo Swift's second shot struck the outline of the heart and he claimed three more points. When Max remained silent and failed to argue the point, Elmo looked surprised, then smug. He was extremely confident that he was going to win.

After Sammy missed the heart by six inches with his second shot, Max took careful aim, told himself to relax—and released. This time, his shot was just outside the outline of the heart. He'd missed by a fraction of an inch.

"Can't give you that one, son," the referee judged. "But it was close."

Elmo leaped in the air, his arms high.

"Hold on, Elmo. It's only the second round," cautioned the referee.

The rest of the shooters were no threat—until it was Marty's turn.

Marty appealed to the referee. "Sir, frankly I stink at this. I may hit somebody else in the heart if I shoot—even you, perhaps. I'm turning my bow over to my friend Susan. She's agreed to substitute for me."

Spectators chuckled as the referee, perhaps thinking Marty's worries about inflicting mortal injury were valid, considered the proposal. Then he nodded his head, permitting the substitution.

Elmo Swift was furious. "Girls shouldn't be allowed," he muttered.

"Here goes," Susan said. She lifted the bow. Phttt! Her arrow thudded right into the middle of the heart and she earned another wild roar of appreciation and a huge ovation.

Elmo Swift slammed down his bow. His vision of

being carried off on the shoulders of his friends, holding his prize aloft, had been shattered. And by a girl!

"Round three!" shouted the referee.

The final round came down to a showdown between Elmo and Susan. Each had two "hearts," so no one else could possibly win.

Elmo went first. Max could see that he was trying to control his anger. Elmo took several deep breaths and stepped to the line. His strong arm muscles rippled as he drew back the bowstring. He released and the arrow slammed into the target—inside the bear but not in the heart. He whooped and hollered. Seven points! Susan had only six points. "You won't get lucky three times in a row," Elmo sneered.

The wind was swirling and the deerskin target began to flap erratically in the breeze. She'd be lucky to hit one of the hay bales.

Susan calmly toed the line. She wasted no time fitting arrow to string. In one fluid motion, she drew the string of sinew back, steadied herself for a split second, gauged the wind and released. The arrow hummed through the air and whacked into the red heart of the bear. Three perfect shots.

Susan was the champion!

Marty hugged her and lifted her in the air. Max and Sammy raced over to congratulate the winner. The crowd waved and cheered. The referee approached her to present the winning prize—an intricate beaded necklace—but because of the celebration, he couldn't get close to her.

Elmo Swift was in a foul mood when his friends tried to congratulate him on his second-place finish. He elbowed them aside, threw his bow to the ground and stalked angrily off into the woods.

There was another test that afternoon—one for the bravest of the brave. It involved a long walk across the trunk of a tree, one that had fallen over the fast-flowing river, just above the falls and the gorge below. Bark had fallen from the log years ago. It was only about eight inches in diameter and a person required great balance, courage and steely determination to make the crossing successfully.

For the powwow, the village elders had ordered a stout rope to be attached to trees at each end of the log, at about eye level, so that competitors would have a better chance to make the crossing. They could hang onto the rope with both hands and pull themselves along. Or, they could use the rope when they faltered or lost courage and turned back. Anyone who lost total balance and tumbled into the gorge 30 feet below would not only get a good soaking, but would risk getting swept into the sharp rocks downriver from the falls. If he swam quickly to shore, he would avoid a second waterfall—an even more dangerous one—100 yards downstream.

"Before we put up the rope, one of our young

men slipped and fell among the rocks and broke his legs," Chief Echo told Max. "Now there's less danger, but this event is not for the squeamish. You going to try?"

"Well, I've tried all the other events," Max replied. "I know this one is a little more dangerous, but count me in."

"I'm going to try it, too," Marty insisted. "I'm not afraid of heights, even though I fell off the roof of a house once."

"You did?" Max asked. "I don't remember that. Were you hurt?"

"Heck, no. It was Mrs. Anderson's outhouse. I went up there to rescue her cat and fell into a snowbank."

Max rolled his eyes at Chief Echo and said, "They're starting the log walking event and Sammy's going to be first."

Sammy walked confidently along the log until he was over the waterfall. He took a quick look at the gorge below and faltered. Clinging to the rope, he fought for balance. The timer yelled out, "30 seconds."

Sammy moved more slowly, more cautiously. Then, he was two-thirds of the way across. He stopped again, took a deep breath and completed the trip, disappearing among the branches of the trees that embraced the far end of the log.

"One minute and 20 seconds is the time to beat," bellowed the timer. His voice could hardly be heard over the roar of the falls.

Three more walkers followed Sammy, but all had difficulty matching Sammy's pace. The rope they clung to swayed back and forth, affecting their balance on the log. Two of them almost tumbled into the gorge below. None was timed in less than three minutes.

Max was surprised to see Elmo Swift take his place on the log.

"I guess Elmo is finished sulking," said Chief Echo. "He's a good log walker. He beat Sammy last year."

Elmo reached for the rope and took several confident steps along the log. Max had to admire his agility and courage. Once or twice he fought for balance, but he didn't look down. He slowed his pace over the treacherous part—the gorge—then finished strongly, scampering nimbly across to the other side and disappearing among the trees.

"One minute and ten seconds," cried the timer. "Elmo's time is the best of the day so far."

"Max, you're next," said Marty, giving his brother a shove. "But I'm coming with you."

"What do you mean?" Max asked.

"I mean... I'll feel better if you walk the log just ahead of me. We'll go together. If anything goes wrong, you'll be there for me."

"Marty, nothing will go wrong if you just hang on to the rope."

"Still, brothers should stick together," Marty insisted.

The timer simply shrugged when Max asked if he and Marty could cross together. "There's no rule against it," he said. "But Max, only your time will count, because you'll be first over. Unless Marty leapfrogs over you to get there first," he added, chuckling.

"I don't care about my time," Marty said. "I just need to prove to myself I can do it."

On the timer's signal, Max and Marty started out, both holding tightly to the rope that swung back and forth overhead. Marty held Max by the belt, making sure he kept close to his brother, who was moving much faster than he'd anticipated.

Now they were over the gorge, and Marty refused to look down. He clung tighter to his brother's belt and realized he was shaking with fear. He could hear the water crashing and tumbling into the rocks below.

Suddenly, the rope they'd been holding came loose in their hands. Both boys froze, tottering on the slippery log.

"Hold on!" howled Max.

"To what?" Marty shouted back. He shot out his arms for balance. But the log was too slippery.

People along the riverbank gasped in horror as Max and Marty fell through the air and tumbled headfirst into the gorge. When Max surfaced, he took a deep breath. Then he looked around for Marty. His brother was still underwater. Max dove deep into the pool, frantically searching for him. His head and chest began to ache. Max needed air. Then he felt something brush against his legs. Max reached down and grabbed his brother around the neck. He pushed hard to the surface and broke it, almost gagging as he gulped air into his lungs. Marty was unconscious and blood flowed from a cut over his ear. Max held his brother's head above the waves that were sweeping them toward the rocks. The brothers crashed into a large boulder and bounced off its side, drawn once again into the swift current. Another boulder loomed up and Max pushed off it with one arm. The other arm was cupped under Marty's chin.

Max realized they were in real danger. There was another waterfall just ahead where the river narrowed. And there was a much smaller pool at the bottom of it. If they were swept over those falls...

"Max! Marty!"

Max shook the water from his eyes and saw Sammy and his pals scrambling over the rocks. They were holding out long poles to assist the brothers. But the falls were also beckoning. Max grasped a pole, but it slipped from his hand. He reached for another and this time was able to hang on. On the other end, Sammy pulled hard, dragging the brothers to shore and to safety. Max felt small pebbles under his feet and stumbled over them, falling to his knees. His grip on Marty never loosened. Then, helping hands were under his arms. Other hands were taking the weight of Marty out of his grasp. Max and Marty were hauled from the brink of the falls and onto soft grass.

"Marty's all right, Max. He's all right," exclaimed Sammy. Relieved, Max leaned his head back on the grass, then everything went black.

CHAPTER 10

FIRE IN THE LONGHOUSE

When Max and Marty showed signs of recovery from their sudden dunking, Sammy and his friends helped them to their feet. Before they staggered away from the river on wobbly legs, Sammy pounded Marty on the back until he coughed up water. Sammy said, "Good boy, Marty. That's a good sign. Now let's get some more water out of you."

He pounded some more and Marty decorated the grass with another copious upheaval. By then, Max was fully conscious.

"You all right, Marty?"

"I guess so. But I swallowed enough water to start a fish pond in my belly. And my head feels like someone's been pounding on it with a hockey stick. I musta struck a rock." He waved a finger at his brother and warned him, "No smart remarks from you about which is harder, my head or the rock."

While Max insisted on walking, Marty was carried

in strong arms to the longhouse, where he was placed on a cot and covered with a blanket. Maude Greentree was there and insisted on taking charge. She examined his cuts and bruises, found no broken bones and said, "I'll have him back on his feet in no time."

"Anything I can get you, brother?" Max asked.

"Yes, there is. You can find the mother of that beautiful girl Susan—the one with the big crush on me. Ask her if she'd let her daughter nurse me back to health."

"Why not ask her yourself, Marty? She's right in front of you."

Marty gasped, turned red in the face and quickly pulled the blanket over his head.

Max and Susan decided to visit the scene of the accident.

"Let's check out the rope across the gorge," Max suggested. "I can't believe it just snapped."

At the river, Susan used her crutch to pull one end of the rope from the water. "Look, Max! It's not frayed. Someone hid in the trees and used a sharp knife to cut it."

Max agreed. "Someone cut the rope when Marty and I were in the middle of the log. We both might have been killed."

"Chief Echo will be really upset when we tell

him," Susan said. "He'll think someone is trying to sabotage the powwow. He'll be disturbed to learn there are enemies among us—even if it's only one."

That night, there was more dancing around the huge fire, and more storytelling too. Marty had persuaded Maude Greentree that his injuries were not serious and she had agreed. When he limped out of the longhouse and over to the fire, he became the centre of attention. People came around to examine his bandaged head, his bandaged arm and his black eye. Little children patted him on the back and told him how brave he'd been.

Marty beamed.

Max asked him if Maude Greentree had given him any instructions.

Marty said, "Yes, she did. She pleaded with me not to break her daughter's heart."

"And you said...?"

Marty sighed. "I said I would try hard not to. But I reminded her that every teenage idol has broken a few hearts in his time. Can't be helped."

Max simply shook his head and rolled his eyes.

Everyone attended the festivities, except Susan, who walked back to the longhouse to rest her sore ankle. When Max and Marty noticed her absence, they went to get her. She told them she was taking some of her mother's medicine to relieve the pain. "I walked too far on it today," she said. "I'll lie down for a little while and join you later."

"I'm surprised Susan didn't ask you to stay with her," Max said to Marty. "You know, hold her hand or something."

"It's obvious she's trying to hide her true feelings for me," Marty answered flippantly. "Girls will do that, you know."

"She's doing a good job of it," said Max dryly.

They returned in time to hear Sammy Fox telling the fascinating story of an Iroquois hunter who, when the world was young, went deep in the woods until he came upon a deep ravine in the dark forest. From the bottom of the ravine, the hunter heard voices and laughter. Curious, he made his way to the edge of the ravine, and then climbed down into the darkness at the bottom.

He was hundreds of feet below sea level. When he reached the bottom, he came upon an amazing sight. Two tiny men, the smallest he had ever seen, greeted him. Each one was about as tall as one of his arrows. He offered the men a small pheasant he had shot and they, in turn, invited him to dinner.

He was amazed to discover a huge tribe of Little People living deep in the ravine. They were an intelligent, powerful race who told the young Iroquois that they controlled all the forces of nature. It was their duty to gently shake the trees and the flowers in the spring of the year, waking them up, and to put them to sleep again in the fall.

These amazing Little People protected all humans from the grip of dreaded underworld figures. "We are small in stature but we are very strong," the Chief of the Little People told the Iroquois hunter. "Watch!" he said, picking up a large stone and hurling it effortlessly at a tree several hundred yards away. The stone hit the tree with such stunning force that it caught on fire, the trunk split in two and branches fell everywhere. The tree was knocked from its roots and fell to the ground, groaning and screaming. Bark from the thick trunk flew in all directions. The hunter was shocked because he had never heard a tree make human noises before.

The Little People fed the hunter food from a bowl that never emptied. He drank a sweet liquid from a cup that was always full. The Little People performed their secret dance—the Dance of Darkness—just for him. He remembered the chants and the movements and when he returned to his village he taught the dance to his own people. He told the villagers that the Little People had promised to come and visit his tribe but they would always be invisible. Their presence could only be felt, not seen.

"Now we will witness the Dance of the Little People," Sammy said. "And when we do, remember the Little People from the deep ravine will fly to our village and share our sacred fire. They will dance along with us, but they are quite shy and will remain invisible. See if you can feel their presence. We always put some food aside for them. Tonight I have placed some food for them on a flat stone near the waterfall."

The dancing began. The people who sat and watched appeared to be mesmerized by the mood, the movements and the beat of the drum. Many looked up and around, sensing there were Little People close by, enjoying the evening as they were.

Suddenly, a restless three-year-old boy jumped to his feet and cried, "I want to see the food." He dashed toward the waterfall. Max leaped to his feet and flew after him; afraid he would topple into the water. Max scooped him up and returned the small boy to his mother, who thanked him.

When Max returned to sit next to Marty, Marty gave him a puzzled look. He said, "Max, what's wrong? You look dazed."

"I am dazed and I'll tell you why. The food Sammy left for the Little People…"

"So? What about it?"

"It was gone!"

Sammy flashed a knowing smile. Then he pulled Max and Marty to their feet. He took them by the hand and inserted them in a line of dancers. While neither could understand the chants, they mimicked the dancers ahead, moving their feet and arms. Everyone was happy to see them take part. When the dance ended, Marty said, "Well, that wasn't so hard. Now I know how to dance."

"Sure you do," Max answered. "When you attend your high school prom someday, your date will be thrilled if that's the only dance you know."

Just then, a loud shriek interrupted the dancing. In front of the longhouse, Mrs. Greentree was jumping up and down, waving and shouting.

"Fire!" she cried, "Fire! The longhouse is on fire! And Susan's inside!"

Everyone leaped up and rushed to the longhouse. The far end of the house was ablaze and the flames were moving fast. Within minutes, the longhouse would be consumed in fire.

Max and Marty were among the first to reach Mrs. Greentree.

"Susan! My daughter." she cried hysterically. "She was asleep. I gave her medicine about an hour ago..."

"Stay by the door, Marty," Max ordered. "I'm going in."

Max rushed through the open door and was immediately engulfed in smoke. Fortunately, he'd toured the longhouse earlier and had a sense of where he'd find Susan. Staying low, he made his way toward her. He was forced to draw in a breath and began to choke on the smoke. He dropped to his hands and knees, crawling as close to the ground as possible.

"Is someone there?" asked a weak voice. "I can't see. I'm blinded by the smoke."

"Susan!" coughed Max. "Susan! Stay where you are! It's me, Max. I'm coming for you."

Through a cloud of smoke, Max glimpsed Susan crouching in a corner, one small fist punching at the wall behind her. Max threw a blanket over her because the flames were coming closer. Already they were lapping at the partition behind her and flaring up from the mats on the floor.

"Oh, Max," Susan cried. "So frightened… I tried to punch a hole in the wall… too strong." Her voice trailed away.

"Shh, you're okay now."

Max scooped Susan up and held her in his arms. Standing upright, he accidentally inhaled more smoke and felt very dizzy. He thought he might faint. In a few seconds the lack of oxygen would surely cause him pass out.

"Hold on, Susan!" he muttered through clenched teeth. He took three short strides, then crouched over like a fullback crashing into the line. He barreled shoulder-first into the wall of the longhouse, holding one arm out to protect Susan so that she avoided the shock of the collision. Max smashed through the partition as Susan screamed. Bark splintered and the wall gave way. Two support poles went flying and the flaming roof began to collapse around them. Large chunks of flaming bark landed with a thud on the dirt floor behind them. Flames and sparks spewed in all directions. By then, Max and Susan were safely out of the longhouse, rolling on the grass. They gulped fresh air into their lungs and then scrambled away from the burning longhouse. Behind the building, Max noticed a number of villagers putting out grass fires, using everything from the blankets they'd been sitting on to garden tools.

People quickly organized a bucket brigade, passing pots full of water from hand to hand, all the way from the river to the longhouse. But it was too late. The pitiful amount of water they threw on the flames had little effect. In 20 minutes, the longhouse was a charred mass of debris.

Chief Echo called his elders together for a meeting.

"A few hours later and we would have been asleep in the longhouse," he said solemnly. "Many might have died. As it is, we lost nobody to the fire. But it was close. Thanks to Max, who braved the smoke and flames, Susan was rescued. We will be forever grateful to you, young man."

Max blushed.

Just then, Sammy burst through the crowd with desperate news.

"What is it, Sammy?" asked Chief Echo.

"Footprints leading into the reserve," Sammy said. "We found them to the north of us." He held up a small metal container. "We also found this. Pulled it out of the grass. Someone tried to hide it."

"But why? What's in it?"

"Gasoline," said Sammy. "Chief Echo, the fire was no accident. Someone set fire to the longhouse on purpose."

"Arson!" said Chief Echo, dumbfounded. "Who would do such a thing? Who would be angry enough to commit such a terrible crime?"

Max had a question.

"Sammy, were the prints you found made by a white man's shoes or were they moccasin prints?"

"Moccasins," Sammy replied. "There's no doubt."

Chief Echo turned to face the group. "Someone on the reserve, possibly someone seeking revenge, was angry enough to destroy our longhouse—with Susan inside. I ask you to help us find that person. He or she must be punished."

The Chief looked forlorn. Sadly he said to Sammy, "I fear our guests will want to pack up and leave now. They will be afraid that other strange things will happen here, bringing harm to their families. We must track down the arsonist quickly. And we must rebuild our longhouse."

The Chief stalked off. Marty shook Max by the sleeve. "Do you think it could be...?"

"I know who you have in mind," Max answered. "Sure it could. Why not?"

CHAPTER 11

SEARCHING FOR ELMO

Max and Marty were talking alone with Sammy. He mentioned once again that moccasins had made the footprints he had found the day before.

"But that doesn't mean that someone from the reserve was responsible," cautioned Sammy.

"It sure doesn't," agreed Max. "The first rule of any investigation is not to jump to conclusions. Consider all the facts. All the possibilities."

Marty piped up. "You guys think Elmo's guilty. Well, I do, too. Sort of."

Max and Sammy exchanged uncomfortable glances. Both would have put Elmo's name on a list of suspects.

"Elmo was pretty angry," Sammy suggested. "It wouldn't be the first time his temper got him into trouble. I've seen him get hotter than Humpty Dumpty after he fell off that wall."

"But Sammy," Marty said. "This was arson. No way Elmo wanted to kill Susan."

"Not deliberately," Sammy agreed. "But maybe he didn't know Susan was in the longhouse. Or maybe he just wanted to scare her. You know, to get even with her for taking first place away from him."

"But Susan won that prize fair and square."

"I know, Marty. But that may not be the way Elmo sees it. Remember, he thought she should have been barred from the competition."

There was a long pause. Then Max said, "What about those Silver City guys? I bet those trouble-makers had a reason to start something."

"You're right, Max. It would have been easy enough for anyone to put on a pair of moccasins to disguise their identity."

"Well," Max said, "right now we better help Chief Echo and the others clean up the fire scene."

Max and Marty found Chief Echo sitting on a large boulder overlooking the waterfall. He was directing the rebuilding of the longhouse and had no time for them. Men and women from all of the tribes hustled back and forth, carrying freshly cut cedar poles, skinned of their bark and trimmed to size. These would form the braces for the new longhouse. Others were deep in the woods, cutting long strips of bark from trees to form the walls and the roof. Still others were mixing a form of pitch—sticky sap from trees designed to adhere one piece of bark to the next. It was amazing how quickly the longhouse was taking shape, and how willing the visitors had been to help. The new longhouse, even longer and wider than the old one, would be ready to be occupied soon—perhaps before dark.

Max and Marty had pitched in, too. Along with Sammy and several other young men, they had toiled from early morning until noon, helping to clear the debris left from the fire. Then the men and women skilled in the ways of building longhouses took over.

Finally, the Chief had ordered a lunch break. Max and Marty took this opportunity to talk to the Chief about Elmo Swift.

"We talked to Elmo's older brother Stoney a few minutes ago," Max said. "Stoney hasn't spoken with Elmo since the log walking event yesterday. He thinks Elmo has run away."

"Elmo and Stoney lost their parents a few months ago," the Chief said with a sigh. "Their parents were picking blueberries alongside the road when a drunk driver from Silver City lost control of his car and ran over them. Elmo has not been the same since. He's still angry and bitter about the verdict in the case. The driver got a suspended sentence. The judge said Elmo's parents must have been wandering in the middle of the road." The Chief snorted. "How many people look for blueberries in the middle of a road?"

The Chief threw a small stone into the pool below the falls. He turned to Marty. "Did Stoney say where Elmo went? And if he's coming back?"

"No, he didn't," Marty answered. "He said he was asleep and woke up to find Elmo was gone. Elmo took his bow and arrows and some food and heavy clothing. Why would he do that?"

"Sounds to me like he's headed for the mountains," Chief Echo said. "Maybe he'll climb over the mountain and live with some of our cousins on the other side. He is still grieving for his parents."

"I think we should go after him," Max suggested. "And try to talk him into coming back."

"If he burned down the longhouse, he *should* be brought back," the Chief said. "He should be punished. If you go, Sammy should go with you. He is an excellent tracker."

"Do we have your permission to go after Elmo, Chief?" Max asked.

The Chief nodded sadly.

"Yes. But wear warm clothing. Bring matches, food and water. Sammy will know what else you will need."

"Will we need a compass, Chief?" Marty asked. "I have one."

"You won't need a compass if Sammy is with you. He never gets lost."

Within the hour, the three friends were following

a trail through the woods. Sammy was in the lead, following moccasin prints in the soft earth. "I'm sure these must be Elmo's prints," he said. "But he's moving fast."

"Maybe he'll go to the ravine where the Little People live," Marty suggested.

Sammy chuckled. "If he finds that ravine, he'll be the first of our people to do so. Did you believe that story I told about the Little People, Marty?"

"It was a good story. Are you telling me it's not true?"

"No. I like to believe it's true. But nobody knows for sure whether or not the Little People exist. Tell me this, did you see anybody take the food we left out for them?"

"No."

"Neither did I. But it was gone, wasn't it?"

"Yep. That's sure a mystery."

"It is, isn't it? One of many in our culture."

There was a stream up ahead. The boys followed Elmo's footprints along the sandy shoreline. Then they leaped from rock to rock to cross the stream. On the far side, they found the footprints again.

Beyond the river, the land sloped sharply upward and became much rockier.

"Look! What's that dark spot on that flat rock?" Max asked.

"It's blood," Sammy said. "Elmo shot a rabbit or a pheasant with his bow and arrow and cleaned it here. Probably a rabbit. I don't see any feathers lying around. That'll be his dinner tonight."

They climbed higher, scrambling over a rocky trail that led up the mountainside.

"Surely he's not going all the way up to the peak," Max said, breathing heavily.

"No, there's a trail that cuts around the mountain about a half-mile ahead of us," Sammy said. "And there's spring water where the trail turns."

Soon they came to a place where the path divided, moving to both the right and to the left of a huge cliff that lay directly in their path. They stopped to dip their cupped hands into a cool spring and drink the water.

"This is where we have to make a choice," Sammy said. "To go left or right. Which way do you think Elmo went?"

"Don't know," Marty answered. "I don't see any moccasin prints. The ground is too rocky."

Max sniffed the air. "Smells like something burning. This way—to the left."

They moved left down the trail for a couple of hundred yards.

"Look!" Max pointed. "The remains of a fire. That's what I smelled." He bent down. "The coals are still warm. Elmo can't be too far ahead of us."

Sammy examined the ground. "Here's some fur. And some bones. This is where Elmo stopped to cook his rabbit dinner."

"We can camp here tonight and pick up his trail in the morning," Sammy said. "Or we can press on for another mile or two. Sun's going down and it'll be dark pretty soon."

"Let's press on," Max suggested. "Try to overtake him before dark."

They set off down the trail, moving quickly through the deepening shadows.

Sammy rounded a bend in the trail when suddenly he dropped flat on the ground.

Whap! An arrow plunked into the trunk of a tree behind him. It had missed Sammy by several inches.

"Hey! Is that you, Elmo?" Sammy called out. "It's me, Sammy Fox. Stop shooting, will you? What are you trying to do, kill one of us?"

"Who else is with you?" called a voice from around the bend.

"I've got the Mitchell brothers with me," Sammy yelled back.

Whack! Another arrow bounced off a nearby rock and ricocheted skyward.

"I'd like to put an arrow through both of them," Elmo called out. "Go back home, Sammy. And take those white faces with you."

"I can't do that, Elmo. Chief Echo told us to bring you back."

There was a brief silence. Then Elmo called out. "Well, I'm not going. I can't go back."

"Why not, Elmo?"

"I did some bad things. I'm too ashamed. Go away. Leave me alone."

Sammy whispered to Max and Marty. "Elmo's voice sounds funny. He should be a long way from here by now. I think he's had an accident and can't move."

"He can still shoot arrows," Marty said. "That first one almost got you, Sammy."

"If he wanted to hit me, he would have," Sammy said. "He seldom misses. It's getting dark. What'll we do?"

"Let me try to reason with him," suggested Max.

Sammy shrugged. "I guess it's worth a try."

"Elmo, it's me, Max Mitchell. I want to talk to you."

A third arrow slammed into the tree.

"Hey!" Max flinched. "Hold on, will ya?" He tried to stay calm. "Listen, Elmo," Max began, "I know you don't like me. That's all right. But you don't want to kill me. Do you really want to spend the rest of your life in jail? Now, I'm going to step around the bend in this trail. If you want to shoot me, go ahead. But I'm relying on you to use good sense not to put an arrow through me. Put your bow down and we'll talk this out."

Slowly, Max stepped into the open.

"Max," Marty whispered urgently. "Don't do this."

It was getting very dark. Max noticed that some large rocks and broken boulders had spilled onto the trail. Max thought he heard a groan.

"Elmo, you okay?"

"I got caught in a rock fall," came Elmo's voice from the darkness up ahead. "Otherwise, I'd have been 50 miles from here by now. It was stupid of you to think you could catch up to me."

"But we did catch up to you," Max said. "And maybe that'll turn out to be a good thing."

From behind a boulder, Max detected the blurred outline of Elmo Swift, an arrow fitted to his bow.

"Are you hurt, Elmo?"

"Yeah, I'm hurt. I almost outran the slide but now my legs are pinned under a pretty big rock. I heard you coming. I shot at you and Sammy but I deliberately shot wide. I thought I'd scare you into turning back. I want to die here. I'm a disgrace to my tribe."

Sammy and Marty had crept along the trail to join Max.

"Put the bow down, Elmo," Max said. "We're coming to help you. Please."

Finally, reluctantly, Elmo lowered the bow. The three boys climbed over the rocks. Elmo was covered with dust. Both his legs were pinned under a huge boulder. He looked bad. "Leg's busted," he muttered. "Left one... careful."

"He's losing consciousness," said Sammy.

"Marty, find a tree limb—a thick one." said Max. "We've got to lever this rock off Elmo's legs."

Marty was back in a minute, a heavy branch under his arm. Carefully, they placed it under the rock.

"I'll get on the end of the branch and pry the rock up. Sammy, you and Marty make sure it rolls away from Elmo's legs. Get your hands under it." Max took a good grip on the branch and shouted, "Now, lift!"

Slowly, the rock moved. It came up, freeing Elmo's legs. He gritted his teeth in pain but he refused to cry out. He pulled his crushed legs away. The boys heaved and the boulder tumbled to the edge of the trail and rolled over, crashing into small shrubs and trees as it bounced down the mountainside.

"There's a flashlight in my pack," Max said. "Get it, Marty." Max examined Elmo's injuries. "His leg's broken, all right," he said.

"We'll need to improvise a splint," suggested Sammy. "And build a fire. We won't be able to walk out tonight."

"Good idea," said Max. "Marty, bring me a gauze bandage from your first-aid kit. We'll put splints on Elmo's leg and wrap it. If you've got iodine in your kit, we'll use it on the cuts."

"There's some flat ground over here," Sammy said. "I'll get a fire going and we'll get Elmo comfortable. Then we'll have something to eat and get some sleep. I'll break off some evergreen branches to put under us."

Early the following morning, cold and hungry, the foursome began retracing their steps. It was difficult getting Elmo over the rock pile, but they managed to carry him across. Marty fashioned a crutch from a tree branch for Elmo when he refused to be carried any farther. "I don't need two white boys to carry me down a mountain," he muttered.

At a bend in the trail, they stopped for a drink of spring water. Suddenly Sammy shouted, "Listen! I hear something."

A frantic Elmo said, "I know that sound. It's another rock slide. Run for it! Leave me here. Otherwise, you'll be crushed."

"No way!" Max shouted. "Sammy, take Elmo by one arm, I'll take the other. Lift him off the ground. Marty, take his crutch. Now let's run for it!"

Hoisting Elmo between them, Max and Sammy hobbled down the trail. Marty trailed behind, dodging a few small rocks that shot past him like shrapnel blown from a cannon. A huge boulder crashed through the trees.

"Look out!" screamed Marty. The boulder crashed into a nearby pine tree, splitting it. Another boulder followed, then a third.

"Faster!" shouted Marty. He looked back and saw boulders bouncing high in the air, careening off one another. They made a noise like giant cymbals. When they plowed into the earth, they crushed trees and bushes.

The boys dodged and weaved, moving as fast as they could. Luckily, the path levelled out and soon the rumble of the falling rocks subsided.

"I think we're okay," Marty shouted. Max and Sammy were trembling with exhaustion. Gently, they lowered Elmo's good foot to the ground. Marty returned the crutch to Elmo.

"Thanks, kid," he said quietly.

Marty smiled. "Hey, no problem. You'd have done the same for me."

"You think so? Well, maybe I would."

They started back down the trail. They were on their way home.

CHAPTER 12
THE LACROSSE CHAMPIONSHIP

A meeting among the elders of the village was held to discuss Elmo. Later, Sammy explained to Max and Marty what happened.

"Elmo told Chief Echo and the elders that he became angry at you, Max, when you showed so much skill at athletics," Sammy said. "He has always been the best. For you, a visiting white boy, to show him up on his home turf—well, it was just too much for Elmo."

"I feel badly, Sammy," Max said. "I didn't know..."

Sammy shook his head. "It's not your fault, Max. Anyway, there was another reason why Elmo acted the way he did. He has this idea that you may be... interested... in a young woman of the village." Sammy raised his eyebrows in mock surprise. "Not true, right?"

Max flushed. "I... er... see, the thing is..." he stammered.

Sammy laughed and raised his hand. "No need to explain, my friend. In any case, Elmo admitted to cutting the rope. He intended to embarrass you by having you fall into the water. He meant no real harm."

"I hope that's true," said Max. "What about the fire in the longhouse?"

Sammy's face became more serious. "Elmo says he was used by the Bradleys. They paid him money and fed him beer to tell them what was going on in our village. He says his tongue became loose and ran off by itself. He told them about our powwow and how the Chief outsmarted the Bradleys by bringing our visitors in through the old trails. He said Blackjack Bradley was furious and said, 'Nobody outsmarts a Bradley, especially a bunch of dumb redskins.'"

"I think it's awful—the names the Bradleys call your people," Marty said angrily. "It's ignorant. There's no excuse for it."

Sammy was silent. Then he said, "Bart Bradley walked Elmo back to the reserve. Bart had a can of gasoline and ordered Elmo to set a torch to the longhouse. Elmo refused. Bart put a gun to Elmo's head and threatened to shoot him. Still he refused. Finally, Bart yanked the moccasins off Elmo's feet and put them on his own feet. While he was busy doing that, Elmo saw his chance and ran away—fast. He found a place to hide in the woods. Bart chased after him, but soon he became winded. He returned and angrily torched the longhouse.

"Elmo was shocked when he saw the flames light up the sky. He panicked, feeling he would be blamed for the fire. So he ran to his longhouse, where his brother Stoney was sleeping. Elmo picked up some new moccasins and supplies and fled up the mountain.

"By the way, he showed a lot of remorse for the way he's acted, the things he's done. He regrets he didn't go straight to Chief Echo and warn him about Bart and the can of gasoline. The Chief has placed him on probation."

Marty yawned. "So what happens next?" he asked. "I think we should get some sleep. It was really late when we got back last night."

"Sleep! There's no time for sleep. Today we play lacrosse again—against the Kickapoos for the grand championship."

Sammy got to his feet and pulled Marty up after him. Marty groaned. "Gee, I'm so tired. Couldn't we play the game tomorrow?"

"Forget it. We're off to the lacrosse field."

A huge crowd surrounded the playing field when the Porcupines faced off against the Kickapoos for the championship.

The barking of dogs caught the attention of the players as they warmed up. A powerful, familiar-looking sled dog was pulling a travois along the path to the lacrosse field.

"What's that thing?" Marty asked. "What's going on?"

Sammy explained that a travois was a device invented by some long-ago Plains Indians and seldom seen in the North Country. It was designed for transporting supplies, and sometimes injured warriors. Two long poles connected at one end were attached behind a horse or a dog and supplies were placed in the middle. The animal—be it horse or dog—could pull a considerable weight and the pulling was easier if the ground was smooth. Travois, pronounced *trav-wa*—was a French name.

Sammy said, "I asked Max if we could use Big Fella to pull ours, and he said sure. Big Fella's the strongest dog I've ever seen." Big Fella spotted Max and Marty and barked out a greeting. It was as if he was telling them he was having the time of his life.

Walking along beside the travois was Stoney Swift. "My brother Elmo pleaded to see the lacrosse match so we used a travois to get him here," Stoney explained. "I think Big Fella could pull two Elmos, he's so strong! By the way, Elmo wants a few words with the redhead—Marty—before the game begins."

Marty was puzzled. *Why would Elmo want to see me?* He said, "Sure, I guess…"

"Not here. At the goal," Stoney said, as Big Fella pulled Elmo to the far end of the playing field.

With the travois parked in the goalmouth, Elmo

asked Marty to stand in the goal. Then, he began to instruct. He talked about the best way to block shots and the easiest way to clear the ball from the dangerous area in front of the net. He even told Marty, "If you charge out and snare the ball, sometimes you'll have clear sailing to the other team's goal. In this game, a goalie can occasionally score a goal. Such a goal can really demoralize the opposing team."

"Thanks, Elmo," he said. "I'm new to this game. I wish I had your skill and experience."

"Good luck," said Elmo. He hesitated. "I'm very sorry for what I did." He reached out his hand. "I'd like to be your friend."

"I'm happy to call you a friend," Marty said. He grabbed Elmo's hand and shook it.

The game began and a constant din was heard as the fans applauded one close scoring play after another. Players raced back and forth with awesome bursts of speed. Some were stopped just as quickly with hard checks that sent them reeling. Max and Sammy performed like they'd been together for years. Max was the set-up man and Sammy was the goal scorer. Before the first half ended, they had combined for three goals. All three were blazing shots that came off Sammy's stick.

Marty was enjoying a marvelous game in goal. He stopped a dozen shots that appeared destined to find a corner of his net and he gobbled up rebounds like a hawk pouncing on field mice. He even earned an assist on Sammy's third goal when he raced to the sidelines, stole a loose ball from a Kickapoo player and fed Max a sharp pass upfield. Max threw the ball on to Sammy. It was just a blur when it flew into the Kickapoos' net.

"Great play, Marty," Sammy heard Elmo shout from the sidelines.

In the second half, Marty was bowled over in the crease by two large Kickapoo players. One gave him a butt end in the ribs as he fell, and the other landed on his upper leg, digging into the soft flesh with his knee. The ball was trapped under Marty's body but the referee, arriving late, ruled it a goal.

Marty got up, holding one arm to his rib cage and limping in pain.

"I don't know whether it was deliberate or not, but they messed me up," Marty told Max. "My ribs hurt and I've got a charley horse. I can hardly move. What's more, the ball didn't go over the goal line."

"Marty, there is no goal line," Max pointed out. "This is just a field. It isn't the big leagues. So we have to accept the referee's decision. But you're hurt. If you can't play, then I'll go in the goal."

Marty tried to laugh but it was more of a grimace. "Max, you're no goalie. You're a goal scorer. I'm the goalie in the family and I won't come out of the game. We've got the lead and less than half a game to play. Ref, blow the whistle. Let's play!"

There was no arguing with Marty. He was determined to carry on, sore ribs, sore leg and a disputed goal notwithstanding.

The players became even more aggressive in the second half. The Kickapoos rained shots at the injured goalie. The inexperienced boy had made them look foolish.

"Those two shouldn't even be on the field," complained the opposing team's coach, pointing at the Mitchells. "They're interlopers, ringers."

"Stop your bellyaching!" warned the referee, who overheard the remark. "For heaven's sake, it's just a game."

At midfield, Sammy was charging when he stumbled over a small stone. The ball popped out of the webbing of his stick and was scooped up by Julian Powless, the Kickapoos' ace player, who flew off in the opposite direction. He drilled a pretty shot past Marty to the upper corner of the net.

The Kickapoo fans leaped in the air, cheering madly. Their team was back in the game. The referee retrieved the ball from Marty's net.

"You okay, kid? You look a little white, if you'll pardon the expression."

"My leg has tightened up, is all," Marty grimaced. "I'll be fine."

After the score, the Porcupines played a defensive game, trying desperately to hold on to their slim lead. With two minutes left to play, the Kickapoos still trailed by only one goal. Dust flew from the feet of the players on both teams as they frantically raced up and down the field. One team was determined to score, the other was just as determined to prevent another goal.

From a faceoff at centre field, Powless snared the ball and passed to a teammate who raced straight toward Marty. The teammate fed Powless a high, looping pass that he took on the dead run. Marty never had a chance. The ball flew into his net and Powless rejoiced, throwing his arms in the air and shouting. The score was tied at three and all the momentum was with the Kickapoos.

Marty hung his head. *If we lose the championship, it'll be my fault,* he told himself. *I can't blame sore ribs and a sore leg for that last goal. I should have had it.* He steeled himself for the final few seconds and wondered if he'd be able to hold himself together through an overtime period.

Again, it was Powless who had a chance to be the hero of the game. He knocked the ball loose from a Porcupine defenceman off to the side of Marty's net. There were 20 seconds left to play. Powless tried to score from a bad angle—and almost did. His hard shot deflected off Marty's quick glove hand and rolled out in front of him. Marty leaped after it. He snared it expertly and tried to pass off to Max. But the ball stuck in the webbing of his stick. He couldn't shake it free, so he sprinted up the field. Suddenly he found himself crossing centre field with most of the Kickapoos in pursuit. There was no time to pass off to a teammate. He would have to try for the winning goal himself. Two Kickapoo defence-men loomed up ahead of him and they were big, tough boys. By then, the ball loosened in Marty's goal stick and he was afraid an opponent would knock it free. Players were hacking at his legs from behind, trying to slow him down. Powless caught up to Marty, breathing heavily, and threw out an elbow, knocking Marty off stride—but for just a second. Powless swung his stick at Marty's goal stick, hoping to pop the ball in the air. But Marty pulled his stick aside and Powless missed.

"Go, Marty, go!" he heard the crowd explode in a mass cheer.

"Four seconds!" someone shouted.

Marty plowed on and plunged right between the two defenders, knocking them aside and warding off their hard stick checks with one arm, protecting the ball with the other. Tears stung his eyes, but he blocked out the pain.

There was only the goalie to beat. *But is there any time left?* wondered Marty. He flew at the goalie, raised his goal stick and ripped a shot low to the corner. The ball kicked up dust as it slammed off the goal post and into the net.

"Score!" screamed the goal judge.

"Game over!" shouted the referee a second later.

He'd done it! Marty had scored the winning goal!

He laughed and threw his arms in the air. Then, his teammates hurled themselves at him.

"You're squishing me," Marty hollered as his teammates avalanched on top of him, laughing and shouting and cheering wildly. He was hauled upright by fans who pounded him on the back. He turned to see Chief Echo and Susan beside him, clapping her hands and shouting "Marty! Marty! Marty!"

Chief Echo winked and whispered in Marty's ear. "It's the Little People, son. They were with you today. Have you ever run that fast before? Have you ever taken such a shot on goal before? It was the Little People who sent you flying down that field like a startled deer."

Marty grinned and shouted, his arms upraised. "Thank you, Little People! Thank you!" The crowd laughed and applauded because they understood.

When Marty left the field with his happy teammates, he came across Elmo Swift, resting in the travois.

"I waited for you, Marty," Elmo said. "You played goal today as well as I ever have. Congratulations."

"Elmo, we both know you're a better lacrosse goalie than I'll ever be." Marty replied. "But I might be a match for you in hockey."

CHAPTER 13
BANJO BILLY LAYS CHARGES

While the Porcupines were celebrating their victory, the roar of a shotgun blast was heard from somewhere in the woods. As if waiting patiently for the lacrosse game to finish, a group of men emerged from the trees.

"It's Blackjack Bradley and his gang," said Chief Echo.

Walking beside the Bradleys was the Sheriff, Billy Bradley. He carried his shotgun with the barrel pointed toward the sky. Smoke curled from its short barrel. In his other hand was a clipboard. Sheriff Billy played banjo in the Bradley Brothers Band, a country music group that was known mostly for playing loudly and off-key. It's how he acquired his nickname "Banjo" Billy Bradley. But people said he cradled his shotgun with more affection than he did his banjo. And he enjoyed making a lot of noise with both.

Ka-pow! Billy fired his shotgun again. When the crowd reacted in near panic, Sheriff Billy grinned like it was the funniest joke in the world. With a toothpick clamped between his yellow teeth, showing a crooked grin, he approached Chief Echo.

"So, Sheriff," the Chief said. "I didn't know you were a lacrosse fan."

The Sheriff moved the toothpick from side to side and sneered.

"I've got better things to do than watch a bunch of redskins chasing after a ball. We've had some serious complaints, Chief. And it's my job to look into them."

Chief Echo ignored the racial slur. "Complaints?" he said. "What kind of complaints?"

"Arson, for one. Burning down your longhouse. That's probably the most serious of the crimes on my list. That calls for a ten-year jail term if we catch and convict the person who did it. I figure it's gotta be one of your people." He pretended to consult his clipboard. "Child endangerment, illegal assembly, serving alcohol to minors. Want me to go on?"

"All lies!" the Chief thundered. "Surely you are joking. And why are all of these other men here?"

"Chief, they're my backup. Everybody knows you can't be trusted to obey the law." He chuckled, and then turned to grin at Bart and Hugo Bradley, who stood just behind him. Bart and Hugo tipped their hats at the crowd and fondled their shotguns. Keeping a low profile, Blackjack Bradley stood behind his two sons.

"Perhaps you'd like to explain how you can justify these preposterous charges and what you are doing on our reserve?" the Chief asked, folding his arms across his broad chest.

"Sure, Chief. First of all, you're holding an illegal gathering—a powwow, you call it. Did you come to me and ask me nicely for a licence to conduct a powwow? No, sir, you didn't. Maybe you forgot. Maybe you think I'm not very important. But I am, Chief, I certainly am important. Then you sneaked all of these people into your village illegally. And they're all guilty of trespassing on other people's property to get here."

"That's ridiculous," the Chief said angrily. "They passed over trails that haven't been used in years. And if they'd gone through Silver City to get here, they would have been hassled and probably assaulted. And you wouldn't have done a thing to stop it. It was a common sense decision we made."

The Sheriff sneered and went on.

"What's more, you and your rowdy visitors have been disturbing the peace with a lot of noise-making and wild dancing. People say it goes on all night! The miners in Silver City can't get their sleep!"

"That's even more ridiculous," Max exclaimed.

"Silver City is a long way from here. The forest absorbs most of the noise. And we're all in bed before midnight."

"Since you're so talkative, Mitchell, let's see what charges we're going to bring against you," the Sheriff stated, looking at the clipboard he carried. "How about kidnapping? And assault? And forcible confinement?"

"What?" Max exploded. "What in the world are you talking about?"

Banjo Bill grinned again. "You were seen chasing Elmo Swift up a mountain and capturing him. Do you deny that? One of our men followed you, thinking you were going to kill poor Elmo. Then there was the brutal assault—breaking Elmo's leg with a boulder to stop him from fleeing. That's clearly assault with a dangerous weapon. You, your brother and Sammy Fox dragged Elmo back here, screaming in pain. Then the Chief confined him to his longhouse."

"We didn't break his leg," Marty spoke out angrily. "That's another lie."

"I wasn't confined," Elmo shouted. "And I didn't scream. A rock fell on my leg."

"Elmo, didn't Chief Echo have someone guarding you?"

"That was in case I needed something during the night—water perhaps. He wasn't a guard."

The Sheriff went back to his list.

"Reckless use of a weapon."

"What? That's impossible. What weapon?" Sammy Fox asked, bewildered.

"Using bows and arrows in a competition, with young children standing nearby. That's mighty reckless, you ask me. Some poor child might have been hit by an arrow. We all know you people can't shoot straight, not like your granddaddys."

Chief Echo sighed. "Our people don't use bows and arrows much anymore, Billy. It was just a friendly competition, to keep the tradition alive."

"Well, you'd best bury some of your traditions, Chief. Begin acting more like us white folks."

"Perish the thought," said a loud voice from the rear.

Chief Echo tried to compose himself. In a voice as calm as he could muster, he asked, "Sheriff, is that the end of your list?"

Banjo Billy almost laughed out loud. He'd been saving the best for last. "No, there's a little matter of attempted murder."

The crowd gasped.

"Attempted murder?" gulped Marty.

"You don't remember, kid?" the Sheriff asked him. "You and your brother almost fell to your death in that gorge. Whoever cut the rope that sent you into the water is guilty of attempted murder. Simple as that."

Incensed at the baseless charges, the crowd muttered angrily. Suddenly, they advanced on the despised Sheriff and his "deputies."

"Here they come, boys!" shouted the Sheriff, raising his shotgun. "Get ready to protect yourselves."

His gang raised their weapons.

Chief Echo stepped forward, holding up his right arm.

"People, don't do anything rash," he ordered. "We all know we are innocent of these charges and we will deal with them. He has no authority here. This is exactly what he wants. Please. Let's all calm down. I command you to back away."

Slowly, the angry crowd retreated. But not before one furious Iroquois spat on the Sheriff's shoe.

It was then that Blackjack Bradley stepped forward. He took off his broad-brimmed hat and waved to the crowd. Nobody was fooled by his display of friendship.

"Folks, I'm really sorry it had to come to this. We have been good neighbours to you folks for many, many years. Believe me, we respect you."

Somebody in the crowd muttered a few words Max couldn't make out.

"What did he say, Sammy?"

"Translation: Bradley's a big, fat liar."

"I'm just trying to help," Blackjack Bradley cooed smoothly. "I don't have any power over the course of justice, since I'm just an average citizen like you."

"Average?" It was another comment from a man in the crowd, but louder now. "That's why they call you the czar of Silver City."

Blackjack ignored his critic. "But I do think Sheriff Bradley, my dear cousin, may have overstated some of the charges he's laid against you good folks. And I think he might be persuaded to drop them all if there was some way of assuring him your shenanigans won't happen again."

"Here it comes," Max said in Marty's ear.

Blackjack Bradley pretended to think. "My suggestion," he said, "is that you find another place for your village. A better place. Why not relocate? Start anew. About ten miles from here is a beautiful valley I happen to own. It's got a lovely lake and the hunting and fishing is good. I'd hate to give it up but the happiness of your people, Chief, is very important to me. We must remember, your people were on this land long before our ancestors arrived."

"Horse feathers!" shouted someone angrily. "Your ancestors drove us off the land. They stole it!"

"That may be, but I'm afraid history can't be changed," Bradley said, with a feigned sigh of regret. "It's really too bad. Anyway, that's my solution to the problem. Chief, why not think about it? If you decide to accept my offer, I'll use all my powers of persuasion to drop all charges against you."

"But moving to another place is a government matter," the Chief said. "Who gives you the authority to speak for the government? Why would the government approve of such a trade?" the Chief asked suspiciously.

Blackjack Bradley shrugged. "I have some friends in high places," he bragged. "And I can be mighty persuasive. Besides, the government has never shown much interest in what happens to your people, has it?"

Good point, thought the Chief.

Playing along with these ridiculous suggestions, he asked Banjo Billy, "How long before we have to make a decision?"

"How about the end of the week?" the Sheriff suggested. "But I want all your visitors to be gone by then. When are they leaving?"

"They plan to leave early Saturday morning."

"Well, today is Thursday, " said Banjo Billy. "Let's see now. That means tomorrow is Friday and then comes Saturday. How about Saturday at noon?"

"That's one smart sheriff," Max murmured to Marty. "He knows at least three days of the week. And he got them all in order."

"I wonder if he knows what day in December Christmas falls on?" Marty said sarcastically.

Something was still troubling Chief Echo. "One more thing, Mr. Bradley," he said. "About that tract of land we argued over a few days ago, the land just north of our village. I say I have a deed to that land. You say you have a deed. How do you propose we settle that?"

"Don't worry about it, Chief," he said, his eyes narrowing. "We both know that land is not good for a dern thing. Maybe we should flip a coin for it. Let's discuss it on Saturday."

"No coin flip," the Chief stated flatly. "I've heard about the white gamblers and their two-headed coins."

Banjo Billy couldn't resist goading the Chief with a final comment about the land in question. "Blackjack's right, Chief. That land you're making such a fuss over is worthless, especially since one of your men threw dynamite in the lake and killed all the fish." He snickered.

"None of my men did that," the Chief retorted hotly. "Whoever did it should be made to swim among the dead fish and pull them from the water one by one with his teeth. Now it's time for you to leave."

"Let's go," the Sheriff said, suddenly anxious to be on his way. His men obediently followed him back into the woods.

"The nerve of those guys," Marty said to Max and Sammy. "The Sheriff talks about trespassing. What the heck were they just doing? Trespassing, that's what. And they've been spying on us all along."

CHAPTER 14

A VISIT TO BRADLEY'S VALLEY

"My ancestors would be ashamed of me," admitted a despondent Chief Echo. "As Chief of my tribe, it is my job to protect my people, to keep them from harm. I let my guard down. Now, some of us may go to jail." He was speaking to the tribal leaders. They had assembled around a fire outside the longhouse. Max, Marty and Sammy hung back at the edge of the assembly.

A swarthy elder named Moses Fishcarrier, Chief of the Mohawks, spoke gently. "Why do you blame yourself, Chief Echo? Because you did not know the men from Silver City were spying on us? Because you did not appoint guards and sentries each night? Those are precautions from the old days, when we were forced to protect ourselves from the white faces. Today, you should not have to worry about spies and sneaks who roam the woods, peeking at our people through binoculars."

"What should I do?" the Chief asked. "With all this trouble, it may be a good thing to move to the land Bradley offers. It is not so far. It would not cause much discomfort."

"Our people have been forced to move too often," objected Chief Whitecoat of the Ottawas. "In the beginning, we welcomed the traders when they came in their canoes. They were *couriers de bois,* 'runners of the woods.' They adapted to our customs and respected our ways. They were good men—most of them, anyway. But then the white man came in greater and greater numbers, taking land as if it were their own. These interlopers did not respect our customs. Some were cruel; many were greedy."

Another wise chief, Billy Bluebird, agreed. "The English and French settlers and soldiers pushed us farther and farther away from the lands we loved. They made us many promises but they kept few. They tricked us with their treaties and they gave us their diseases. Were our ancestors supposed to say, 'Thank you, white man, for your wonderful gift of smallpox—we'll never forget it?'" the old man snarled angrily.

The assembled elders applauded Billy Bluebird. He turned to Chief Echo.

"To you and your people, Chief Echo, I say, if you love this land, stay on it. Fight for it, if necessary."

Another elder, still mulling over Billy Bluebird's

remarks, snorted and said, "Have you heard the story of the three runners? It proves how devious the newcomers to our shores became. Shortly after they arrived, one of our chiefs agreed to sell the white faces some land, as much land as a man could cover in a day. He did not think it would be very much. But the white faces cleared a path and brought in three fast runners. One started running just after midnight. When he dropped of exhaustion, a second runner took his place. Then it was the third runner's turn. When the third runner finished and the day was over, the pale faces laughed and laughed. They had three or four times as much land as the old chief thought they would have. When the chief argued that it was unfair, that the spirit of the agreement had been broken, they laughed at him some more and offered him a bottle. 'Here are your spirits,' they said. And when he continued to complain, they smashed the bottle and said, 'Agreements can be broken as easily as a glass bottle.'"

"There are many stories like that," agreed Chief Echo solemnly.

There was a period of silence while the elders passed around a long peace pipe. Finally, Chief Moses Fishcarrier said to Chief Echo, "My noble friend, do you know anything about the land that lies ten miles from here? It could be swampland, home to a million mosquitoes. It could be land that fire has laid bare of trees. It could be a land where deer are scarce and skunks are common. Is Bradley telling the truth when he says it is beautiful land?"

"I don't know if he is being truthful. I have not been to that place for some time," the Chief answered. "But I will find out. I will send Sammy and his friends to walk that land."

After the assembly, Chief Echo called for Sammy Fox and Max to come forward.

"Yes, sir?" asked Sammy.

The Chief put his large hand squarely on Sammy's shoulder. "Tomorrow morning, I want you and the Mitchell brothers to walk the land that Bradley has offered to us. Look it over carefully. Then, I need you to take Max and Marty to Indian River. Use the DeSoto. We must find out more about Bradley's offer. Find out from Max's father if he has made any headway in his investigation. He may know more about the dispute over the deed. Take Susan with you. She is very bright. She will prove helpful. Find out all you can."

The Chief turned to Max. "What do you think, Max? Would a fellow like Bradley keep his word?"

"Not for a minute," Max said. "He should be trusted like the hawk who says to the baby rabbit, 'Let me take you in my beak and give you a nice ride in the air.'"

Early the following morning, the old DeSoto nosed its way onto the main road toward Indian River. Villagers with shovels had filled in the hole made by the dynamite blast.

"Where'll we go first, Max?" Sammy asked. "Meet with your dad in Indian River or go the other way, through Silver City and on to the land the Chief wants us to look at?"

"Turn right, Sammy," Max said. "Let's meet my dad at his newspaper office. I called him and he's expecting us. Then we'll double back and go through Silver City."

Harry Mitchell was delighted to see his sons and their friends when they arrived at his office. He said, "Let's go down to the Merry Mabel's for a snack." He was pleased to meet Susan, who was walking almost normally now. "How did a bright young woman like you get hooked up with these three troublemakers?" he asked her jokingly as they entered the restaurant, hiding his wink from the boys.

"I'm here to try to teach them some table manners," she answered, her eyes twinkling. "And to try to keep them out of trouble, which seems to be more and more difficult all the time. It seems to follow them everywhere."

She turned to whisper in Harry Mitchell's ear. "Actually, your sons are really popular with the villagers. You might not get them back."

"Hooray!" yelled Harry in mock delight.

"What was that, Dad?" Max asked.

"Nothing, son. Nothing." His father answered, smiling.

They ordered sandwiches with fries and soft drinks. Then Harry Mitchell got down to business.

"I thought I'd have some good news for you today. But I'm sorry, I don't. Earlier today, I got a call from a friend of mine who works in the deeds office in Capital City."

"And?" said Max, leaning forward in his chair. His father looked him in the eye. "Max, there are no documents, no records at all of that deed."

"But there have to be," Max argued. "It had to be registered, right?"

"Right. And filed away," said his father. "But when my friend searched for the file, it was missing. He said files sometimes go missing, but they usually turn up. He said he searched everywhere."

"That's not good news. The file was lost?" asked Marty.

"Not lost, Marty," said Mr. Mitchell. "I think it was stolen."

"Stolen!"

Mr. Mitchell nodded. "When I was on the phone with my friend, I asked him if anyone named Bradley had ever worked in his office. He said he couldn't recall an employee by that name. I was about to hang up when he said, 'Wait a minute, Harry.' He wasn't positive, but he thought he remembered that his secretary many years ago—a red-haired girl named Myrtle—might have been stepping out with a fellow named Bradley."

"Stepping out?" asked Marty. "What the heck is that?"

Mr. Mitchell smiled. "It means dating, son. Anyway, he said she got married and moved to some town in the North Country, a mining town named Silver City, a long time ago."

"You think Bradley told her to steal the government copy of the deed?" asked Max.

His father nodded. "I believe it's likely that Blackjack Bradley had Myrtle steal documents dating way back, with the intent to someday take ownership of property around the North Country."

"We can't prove that Chief Echo's band held that land," said Susan, sadly. "It's his word against Blackjack Bradley's."

"I'm afraid it looks that way."

Max, Sammy and Susan were eager to go. But Marty kept them waiting while he polished off a giant banana split.

"Come on, Marty," Max said. "It's getting late. We've got to be on our way."

In his haste to finish, Marty spilled a sizeable portion of the ice cream down the front of his shirt. He was still wiping it off when his father paid the bill.

The four teens drove north, the DeSoto clipping along at 40 miles an hour. They had many miles to cover before the day was over.

"Wow! This is some speed, isn't it, Susan?" hollered Marty from the back seat, his hair whipping in the breeze.

Suddenly, Sammy saw another car approaching from the rear and travelling fast—a big Ford kicking up a huge cloud of dust. Sammy slowed to let it pass and when it did, he saw the Bradley brothers, Bart and Hugo, in the front seat. Hugo rolled down his window when the Ford roared alongside. He yelled at Sammy, "You stupid fool. Where'd you learn to drive? You're throwing dust in our faces. We can hardly breathe. Now we'll give you a taste of yer own medicine."

The Ford cut directly in front of the DeSoto and slowed. Dust came in from all sides and Sammy could barely see through the windshield. Max covered his mouth with his handkerchief. He could hear Marty and Susan coughing in the rumble seat. When Sammy slowed, the Ford slowed. After a mile or so, Sammy gave up. He pulled the DeSoto to the side of the road and stopped. The Ford raced away and raucous laughter filled the air.

"Those Bradley boys have a weird sense of humour," Max observed as he dusted himself off.

"I must look like a mummy," Susan said. "I'm covered in dust."

When the dust settled, they got back in the car and drove on. Sammy slowed down to 25 miles per hour through Silver City. He didn't want any more trouble.

On the other side of town, he sped up again and soon they reached the boundary of Bradley's land.

Max got out the map and suggested they split up into two teams.

"Marty, you and Susan go in that direction," he said, pointing. "Sammy and I will go this way. We'll meet back here at the car in, let's say, two hours."

The four teenagers entered the woods and followed stakes set in the ground every few yards to mark the boundaries of the valley.

Two hours later they met back at the car.

"Well, what do you think?" Max said, looking first at Marty and Susan.

"It's a beautiful place, all right," Marty said. He swiped at his muddy clothes. "I fell over a log and into a creek," he explained. "And I stepped in some poison ivy. I ran from a skunk and I've got burrs in my hair. But it was a lot of fun."

"I would have thought the skunk would have run from you," Max said. "Especially if that internal gas machine you like to show off was in good working order."

"Never mind that, brother. Can't you see there's a lady present?"

"We saw lots of wonderful old trees and a small lake with trout in it," Susan added, pretending she hadn't heard. "They were jumping for flies."

"We saw some beautiful scenery too," Sammy said. "And some great soil for farming. Looks like Blackjack Bradley told the truth about this place. If we do decide to move, we can't go wrong with this valley."

"It's almost too good to be true," said Sammy suspiciously.

"Let's start back," Max suggested. "There's a gas station about a mile down the road. We'd better gas up and get some oil."

At the gas station, Max chatted with the owner, a talkative man named Cecil Prendergast. He said he'd seen them earlier, going in the other direction. "Haven't seen a DeSoto like that in years," he said. "Headed back to Silver City, are you?"

"That's right," Max said. "We've been out at the Bradley property."

"That so?" said Cecil. "Beautiful land. Too bad it won't be that way much longer."

"What do you mean?" asked Max.

"My brother Elmer's in the lumber business," Cecil said. "He was in here the other day. Said he bought the logging rights to that property from

Blackjack Bradley. He told me not to talk about the deal, but I guess it won't do no harm to tell a few kids about it. In a few months, when he finishes his business up north, my brother will be taking a hundred logs a day off that property. That valley is gonna be a desert when he finishes. Good thing you tramped through it today. It'll never be that beautiful again."

Max bought four soft drinks and they left.

It was silent in the car until Sammy said, "I knew it was too good to be true. Blackjack Bradley lied to us. In a few months, there won't a tree left standing in that valley. It'll look like a war zone."

Max stared stonily through the windshield.

"Don't worry, Sammy," he said. "He's not going to get away with it. We're going to stop him."

CHAPTER 15

ARRESTED IN SILVER CITY

The DeSoto lurched along the dirt road, emitting a cloud of blue smoke from its tailpipe. Sammy pulled over once, opened a can and poured a quart of oil into the engine. Then, he noticed steam beginning to hiss from the radiator. He waited until the engine cooled off, went to a nearby ditch, filled a gallon can with water and poured it slowly into the radiator, which burped and gargled noisily as it swallowed the water.

"She was hungry for oil and thirsty for water," Sammy said with a chuckle. He closed the hood and patted it. "Good girl," he said, gently. "Now just keep the air in your tires until we get back home."

"Sammy, pat her again," Susan said. "And say 'please.' She likes affection and good manners."

Laughing, Sammy patted the hood once more and said, "Please, sweetheart, be a good girl today. We love you and want you to live forever."

He got back in the car, wiped his hands on a rag he pulled from under the seat and drove on toward Silver City.

It was a good time for Max to talk to his friend Sammy.

"Marty and I have learned a lot about the Indian way of life since we came here to visit you," Max said. "But why do men like the Bradleys resent you and your people? Why all the anger?"

"Guess I'll never understand it," Sammy said. "That's why having white friends like you and Marty is so important to me. It makes up for any number of ignorant Bradleys."

"Are there any famous athletes among your people?" Max asked.

Sammy smiled and said. "Growing up, my first sports hero was Tom Longboat. He was a Canadian distance runner, the best in the world. He came to visit our reserve once a couple of years ago and I got his autograph."

"I don't know much about him," Max confessed.

"He was an Onondaga from the Six Nations Grand River Reserve. He showed up for his first marathon race in Hamilton, Ontario, wearing a ragtag bathing suit and old sneakers, and people laughed at him. But he won that race easily despite the odds of 60-1. He won the Boston Marathon in 1907 in record time. They called him 'The Golden Mercury.' He might have won the gold medal in the 1908 Olympic Games, but he collapsed during the race from the intense heat. Later, he won the World Professional Marathon at Madison Square Garden in New York City. He was a runner in France during the First World War, racing between battalions with important messages. He was wounded twice and left for dead once. It was dangerous work. Somehow he survived. But when he returned home, his wife, thinking he'd been killed in the war, had married another man. He spent the last few years of his life working as a garbage man."

"Do you have another sports hero?" Max prompted.

"My other favourite was an all-round athlete: Jim Thorpe."

"I've heard of him," Max said. "He was an Olympic champion, wasn't he?"

"One of the greatest," Sammy said proudly. "After he won gold medals in both the pentathlon and decathlon in Sweden—that was in 1912—the King of Sweden called him 'the greatest athlete in the world.' He played both professional football and professional baseball. He was from Oklahoma—a member of the Sac and Fox tribe."

"Did you ever meet Jim Thorpe, Sammy?" Marty asked.

Sammy smiled and said, "No, but I met Pinto."

"Pinto? I've never heard of him," Max said.

Sammy feigned a look of surprise. "You haven't? Well, I met Pinto when he was a little boy learning to play baseball. The pitcher on the opposing team, feeling sorry for the lad, walked Pinto on four pitches. The coach at first base told Pinto, 'On the next pitch, run as fast as you can to second base.' And Pinto did. Then he ran to third base on the following pitch. When he stood on third base, huffing and puffing, the third base coach told Pinto, 'If the batter hits the ball, run home fast and slide in hard.' When the batter hit the ball, Pinto took off. He ran through the field and across the bridge and he ran all the way to his longhouse. There he flew through the door, sliding hard and surprising his mother.

"She said, 'Pinto, I thought you were playing baseball today.'

"He said, 'I am, Mom. I just made a run.'"

Groans and laughter filled the car.

Suddenly, Max pointed through the dusty windshield.

"What's that up ahead?" he asked Sammy. They were approaching Silver City and Max had noticed something—or someone—in the middle of the road.

They drew closer and Sammy said nervously. "It looks like the Sheriff and he's waving us down. It can't be for speeding. I'm only doing 25 miles per hour."

Sammy pulled to the side of the main street. The

Sheriff approached the DeSoto, a toothpick hanging from his lip.

"Well, well, well," the Sheriff said, leaning in the car window. "Don't you fellows care anything for the safety of our dear little children in Silver City? Or the senior citizens we love to serve and protect?"

Max looked around. There was not a child in sight. Nor were there any old people.

"What do you mean, Sheriff Bradley?" Sammy said politely.

"I mean we got laws against tearing through town at breakneck speed. You'd think you were headed to the Indianapolis Speedway." His voice grew hard. "You were speeding, is what I mean. Ten miles an hour over the limit, at least. I gotta give you a ticket for that. It'll cost you five dollars." The Sheriff stood back, hands on his hips, staring impatiently.

"Sheriff, believe me, we weren't speeding," Sammy said. "I was very careful to make sure I was under the limit."

"And I'm saying you were over the limit. Well over it."

Max leaned across Sammy to make a point. "But how could you tell my friend was speeding? You were standing in the road ahead of us."

Banjo Billy's eyes narrowed. The toothpick moved back and forth in his mouth. He pointed to his eyes and spat out, "I've got 20/20 vision, boys. I can tell just by looking at a car how fast it's going. That's all the proof I need. You want to argue with me? It'll cost you even more money."

Max and Sammy huddled in the front seat, trying to decide what to do. Meanwhile, a group of Banjo Billy's pals emerged from the town's saloon and gathered around, enjoying the show.

"I heard you boys got a little dusty today," Hugo Bradley called out. "Har, har, har."

Max told Sammy they'd better avoid a confrontation and get out of town, even if the speeding ticket was outrageous.

"Give us the ticket, Sheriff," he said. "Sorry we don't have five dollars with us. We'll come into town and pay it tomorrow."

"No, you won't. You'll pay it now—on the spot. You take off and I'll never see you again."

"But you'll see us tomorrow." Max said, totally frustrated. "You know us. We promise…"

"He wants the five dollars to put in his pocket," Susan said quietly. "He doesn't give out actual tickets. And no receipts. That's how he makes his income. Most people don't want the hassle so they pay what he demands and move on."

Banjo Billy shot her a look. "That's enough out of you."

Susan jumped down from the rumble seat, her eyes blazing.

"You may be a lawman but you're also a nasty little twerp," she exploded. "And you're a bully and a cheat and a disgrace to the law. And a coward, I'll bet. You'd be afraid of your shadow if you didn't have a bunch of drunken losers to back you up."

"What was that you called us, honey?" Hugo called out indignantly.

The Sheriff uttered a mean little laugh. "I just remembered something, toots," he said. "You tell your friends that speeding through town calls for a ten-dollar fine—not five." The men loitering outside the saloon roared at his remark and slapped their knees. "That's tellin' the little wildcat," Hugo hollered.

His brother, Bart, did a little dance. "The man said ten dollars. Do I hear 15, 15 dollars?" Bart sang out, imitating an auctioneer. A skinny woman with red hair matching her red lipstick held Bart by the arm and laughed hysterically. "Bart, you are so funny. You should be on the stage."

"That must be Myrtle Bradley," Sammy whispered. "Blackjack's wife. The file thief."

The Sheriff waved a hand, calling for less wise-cracking. "Young lady, 15 dollars is what I fine people who assault a policeman while doing his solemn duty. That's what you'll have to pay me."

Susan was irate. "But I didn't assault you," she cried. "I never touched you. I just called you..."

"I heard what you called me. And that's assault—verbal assault," interrupted the Sheriff. "Why, it's almost the same as hitting me over the head with a sledgehammer."

"I'd love to see that," Hugo hooted. "I'd love to see which would break first, your head or the sledgehammer. Har, har, har."

Marty couldn't hold back any longer. He stood nose-to-nose with the Sheriff, saying, "You're the most pitiful excuse for a sheriff I've ever seen. It's about time someone like Susan told you exactly what you are. We're not paying some imaginary fine you just figured out in your head. We're outta here."

Marty turned, but a firm hand on his sleeve pulled him back. He felt a handcuff slip around his left wrist and heard a clicking sound. Susan reached out to pull Marty away and her right wrist was quickly surrounded by a metal handcuff. "There now," the Sheriff snickered, "Got you both. Banjo Billy strikes again!" The crowd outside the saloon hooted and hollered. Some of them applauded. Banjo Billy acknowledged them by doffing his hat and bowing from the waist.

Seeing his brother handcuffed to Susan was more than Max could bear. He leaped out of the car, followed by Sammy. But they found themselves staring into the barrel of a revolver Banjo Billy had pulled from a holster. Outside the saloon, a couple of shotguns appeared as if by magic in the hands of Hugo and Bart.

"You boys get right back in that bucket of bolts you call a car and get out of here," the Sheriff demanded. "Get back here tomorrow and bring some money to pay your fines."

"All right," said Max, feeling the battle was lost. "No need to point guns at us. Take the handcuffs off Marty and Susan and we'll go. Come on, Marty, Susan. Get back in the car."

"Not so fast," sneered the Sheriff. "I'm keeping these two in jail overnight. Both of them verbally assaulted me. Now they're going to find out what it's like to spend a night in the Silver City jail. One cell, one meal and one blanket each. No bail, no visitors and nobody to cheer them up but the bedbugs." He began to lead Susan and Marty away. Then he turned to Max and Sammy, "Now scat! Get out of town before Bart and Hugo shoot a bunch of holes in that rusty old heap."

"That would be against the law," Max protested. "You'd have to arrest them if they did that."

Hugo raised his shotgun and fired a blast that kicked up dust in front of the DeSoto. Bart followed suit. "Now Banjo Billy's gonna have to put us in the slammer, right, Billy?" Hugo hollered.

"Not today, Hugo," the Sheriff replied. "There's no law against having a little fun. And you didn't come close to putting that old flivver out of its misery."

The Sheriff led Susan and Marty away, smirking as he passed the crowd outside the saloon. He turned down a side street and pushed his captives through the door of the town jail. Inside, there was one small cell with four metal cots in it. Two of the cots were occupied.

"They're the town drunks," Banjo Billy explained. "Mort and Lefty. They're harmless. They just like to fight with each other ever' once in awhile. Last night I had to charge them with being drunk and disorderly. Listen to 'em snore. You can hear 'em over the scream of the sawmill down the street. I should wear earmuffs in here." He rattled his keys and yelled through the bars. "Hey, you knuckleheads, you gonna sleep all day?" Neither man stirred.

He used a large key to open the cell door, and then growled at Marty and Susan. "Get in there!"

"I'm not going in there," Susan protested. She held a finger under her nose. "They stink!"

"She's right," Marty said. "They smell like a garbage dump. I'll go in but you can't put Susan in there. Not with those bums."

"You'll get used to it," the Sheriff said, pushing first Marty, then Susan through the cell door. "I told you they're harmless." He slammed the door behind them and locked it with the large key.

"Now put your arms through the bars and I'll take

off the cuffs," he ordered. They did so and after pocketing the handcuffs, the Sheriff sniffed the air and declared, "You're right. It smells like a convention of skunks in here. I guess I'll get me some fresh air. I'll be back in awhile. Goin' to dinner," He turned and stalked toward the front door.

Susan looked nervously at the two other inmates.

"What if they wake up?" Susan asked. "I don't believe you when you say they're harmless. You can't leave us with these two low-lifes."

Banjo Billy laughed. "They won't wake up. I'll be back before you know it."

Banjo Billy was hardly out the door when one of their cellmates stirred and sat up. He threw off the tattered blanket that covered him. Underneath, he was fully dressed. He hadn't even removed his muddy boots. His face was scratched and covered in dried blood. He looked like he'd never seen a bathtub or a bar of soap. His trousers and shirt looked as old as the century. He looked around him and saw Susan and Marty sitting on the edge of the bunk across from him.

"Well, well, well, what have we here?" he said in a hoarse voice. "Visitors? I don't think I know you two."

"We're not visitors," Marty replied. "We're inmates. But not for long."

The man roared with laughter loud enough to

wake the man in the upper bunk. "Wasgoinon, Mort?" the second man mumbled, leaning over the edge of his cot, his mouth open, his long greasy hair falling over his eyes. His face also was marked by several cuts and scratches and he had two black eyes.

"We've got visitors, Lefty," the man named Mort replied. "And one of them's an Indian gal."

Mort slid heavily off the bunk, pulled his red suspenders up over his shoulders and stood tottering as he glared at Susan. He was about 40 years old, balding, short, fat in the stomach and bow-legged. Susan turned her head away. The man's breath reeked and his body odour was repugnant. *It's men like these who are always first to use that phrase "dirty Indian,"* she thought.

Mort motioned to his cellmate, Lefty, to come and join him. When Lefty stood next to him, the odour was doubly disturbing.

"Now let's get down to business," Mort said, his voice taking on a less friendly tone. "How much money you kids got?"

"Yeah. We need some cash," grinned Lefty through a mouth of missing teeth.

"We've got no money," Marty fibbed, looking Mort straight in the eye. Marty had hidden all his money—a five-dollar bill—in his shoe, immediately after being thrown in the cell.

Mort snorted. "Liar. Search him, Lefty." He leered

at Susan. "I'll check this gal."

Mort grabbed Susan by both arms. It was a huge mistake—like putting his hand on a lioness. Susan leaned back hard, pulling her attacker off balance. Then she struck out with one foot, kicking Mort hard between the legs. He howled in pain and dropped to the floor hard, as if he'd fallen down a flight of stairs.

Marty tried a similar tactic on Lefty, and the other man sprang back—but not before taking Marty's kick to a tender spot behind the knee. Lefty cried out, reached down and cradled his knee with both hands, as if he thought it might jump up and run away. Marty leaped on him and knocked him backward. Lefty fell and cracked his head against the cement floor. Mort and Lefty lay there, moaning and groaning.

Marty waved his Boy Scout knife, its short blade flashing in the air.

The blade made Lefty very nervous. "Don't stick me, kid," he pleaded. "My head hurts. I don't want no trouble. And I faint if I see blood." He staggered to his feet and fell back on the cot behind him, pulling his knees to his chest, folding like a road map.

"Susan," said Marty. "Take Mort's boots off and pull out the laces. Do it now, before he recovers. Use the laces to tie his hands together behind his back. Then tie his ankles together. I can help by stepping on his neck while you do it." Marty placed a foot on Mort's neck, producing a squawking sound from his victim's gaping mouth. Susan worked at the laces, quickly and quietly. *She's a brave girl,* Marty thought. *Very cool under stress.*

Next, Marty turned to Lefty. He ordered him to turn over on his stomach. Lefty complied meekly, afraid of Marty's knife. "Don't stick me, kid," he whined. Susan then tied Lefty's arms together behind his back and wrapped his shoelaces around his ankles, knotting them tightly.

"Now we'll pick Mort up and put him back in his bunk," Marty said.

"The upper bunk? He's too heavy. We'll never get him up there," Susan said.

"No, the lower one. We'll squeeze them in it together. Since they're cousins and best pals, I think they'd like to be together. It'll be cozy."

When the two drunks were placed in the lower bunk and lay nose to nose, Lefty muttered to his pal, "Now, look what a mess you got us into, Mort. If my hands were free, I'd haul off and sock you."

Mort tried to turn his head away. "Aw, shuddup," he said. "I can't stand your stinkin' breath."

From the other side of the cell, Marty and Susan studied their two would-be attackers.

"How are we going to explain all this when the Sheriff comes back?" Susan asked.

"Don't know," Marty replied, folding his knife and putting it back in his pocket. "We'll tell him the truth, I guess. My dad says you can hardly go wrong when you tell the truth. The Sheriff should never have left us alone with these two creeps in the first place. Who's to say he won't untie them? Then we'll be right back where we started."

CHAPTER 16

THE JAILBREAK

Max and Sammy drove the DeSoto back to the village of Tumbling Waters and told their story of the events in Silver City. Maude Greentree was distraught when she learned about her daughter's arrest. "You mean to tell me my Susan was thrown in jail? And Marty, too? Sammy, turn that car right around! Take me in to Silver City. I'll tell that Sheriff a thing or two. I'll put a hex on that, that, that… imbecile of a man."

Sammy whispered to Max. "I've never seen her this angry before."

"With good reason," Max agreed.

Chief Echo was mulling over the events of the day, as related to him by Max and Sammy. "As much as I think it was shameful, even illegal, for Banjo Billy to arrest Susan and Marty, I don't think we should go back to Silver City today," he said. "Bradley's gang will be expecting us and they have shotguns, rifles and pistols. We have only a couple of hunting rifles in the village. We certainly don't want to get involved in a shootout. There've been more than enough of those in our past. If real trouble breaks out, there's no telling what those thugs might do."

"So it all comes down to tomorrow at noon," Max said. "And your visitors to the powwow are leaving for home early in the morning. So we'll be on our own if there's trouble with the Bradleys."

"Yes. Blackjack Bradley is hoping I'll agree to move the tribe to the valley you visited today. He's a smart man, Max. He must know something about Tumbling Waters that we don't know, something that we haven't noticed, because we are sitting right on top of it every day."

Max looked around. "What could it be, Chief Echo? This appears to be land that is no better, and no worse, than any other land."

"I think he and his gang just want to be rid of us," Sammy said, looking annoyed. "He's turned all the people in Silver City against us. I think it's an issue of prejudice against our people and nothing else."

Max had a final question. "Do you know what your answer will be tomorrow, sir?"

"No, I will sleep on it." He gave Max a sly smile. "Maybe the Little People will enter my dreams and tell me the wise thing to do."

Max walked back to his longhouse. He thought of

what the Chief had said about Blackjack Bradley's motives. Perhaps there is something here in the village; trees for lumber, maybe, or fresh water. *Something we haven't noticed because we're sitting on it.* Chief Echo's words kept ringing in his head.

There was a small wooden box in the longhouse, filled with socks and shirts. Marty's stuff. Marty's bathing suit was on top of the box. Max moved it aside so he could sit on the box and think. Under the bathing suit was a rock, the rock Marty had slipped into his pocket when he and Max were hiding from Sammy and his Indian pals.

Max tossed the rock from hand to hand. He rolled it around in one hand. Then he held it up to the light from the setting sun that blazed in through the opening to the longhouse. He studied the rock for a long time, turning it this way and that. Then he laughed, kissed the rock and put it in his pocket. Smiling, he picked up Marty's latest Hardy Boys book.

He decided to read for a few minutes, waiting until dark. The Hardy Boys had worked themselves out of every kind of problem, every conceivable dilemma. They were experts at finding clues and determining who were the good guys and who were the bad guys.

Max didn't have a clue as to how to deal with Blackjack Bradley. If he read a few pages of the Hardy Boys, maybe he'd find one.

He waited for the sun to go down.

When it fell beyond the horizon, he dressed in dark clothes and went to find Sammy. His friend was at the powwow. It was the windup dinner with music and dancing on this night. Everyone was having a wonderful time. Chief Echo had been successful in keeping his problem with the Bradleys—and the arrest of Susan and Marty—away from most of his guests. He had confided in the other chiefs and leaders but no one else. He didn't want to spoil their evening.

Max and Sammy were talking in whispers when Maude Greentree came up to them. She was very agitated, fighting back tears.

"Sammy and Max, I need your help," she pleaded. "I must respect Chief Echo's decision to avoid a battle with the Bradleys. But I can't bear the thought of that arrogant Sheriff holding my Susan overnight. There may be only one cell in that jail, two at most, and if the Sheriff arrests a drunk tonight—or two or three drunks—he may toss them in the cell holding Susan. That would be intolerable. I worry about Marty, too. He's too young to be thrown in jail."

Max nodded. "I worry about them both. But you're right about Susan. I have a plan, but I need Sammy's help. We can't leave Susan and Marty there overnight."

He told Sammy and Maude Greentree what he had in mind.

"We'll be taking a big risk," Sammy said after much consideration. "We could all wind up in that stinking jail. And Chief Echo may be furious with us when he finds out." Sammy looked gravely at his friend, and then broke into a determined grin. "You know what I think?"

"What?"

"I think we should do it!"

It was pitch dark when Max and Sammy parked the DeSoto behind some cedar trees on the outskirts of Silver City. It was after ten o'clock and many of the residents were already in bed. But there was plenty of noise coming from the saloon—a piano playing, boozy conversation and riotous outbursts of laughter. Surely the Bradley brothers would be there. Max and Sammy slipped unseen through back streets until they came to an alley alongside the town jail.

"I'll take a look, Sammy," Max whispered. "You wait here."

Max glided around the corner and peeked in the front window of the building. In a room to one side, he saw Banjo Billy sitting in a rocking chair. He appeared to have fallen asleep while listening to a radio.

On the other side of the jail was a small cell. Max could see his brother and Susan. Susan was sitting on the side of a cot, looking forlorn. Marty was pacing the cell. Max saw Marty walk over to the cot

165

opposite from Susan and look down at what appeared to be a sleeping body—a big one.

Max retreated into the shadows. He pulled something over his head—a gruesome mask painted to resemble a mountain lion. Sammy handed him a long staff—a spear with a sharp end painted bright red. Sammy then pulled something over his body and pronounced himself ready.

They tiptoed to the front door. It was unlocked and opened easily. They stepped inside. In the odious cell, Marty and Susan heard the soft sound of the door clicking open and looked over in astonishment. Max put his finger to his lips, then motioned for Sammy to follow him into the Sheriff's office. Max paused a moment inside the door, clicked off the overhead light, then hissed like a snake as he poked the spear into Banjo Billy's belly, just hard enough to knock some of the wind out of him. Sammy, wearing the bear costume, stood up, placed a large paw on the Sheriff's arm and growled.

"Aaaarrrgghhh!"

Banjo Billy's eyes flew open. He would have screamed in terror if Max hadn't clapped one hand over his open mouth. Eyes bulging, the Sheriff fell backwards out of the chair. He began to sob.

"Don't make a peep!" Max said, his voice a husky growl. "Or my bear will chew your leg off."

"I won't. I won't make a peep," cried the Sheriff.

"Please don't hurt me. Take my money."

"Just give me the keys to the cell," Max growled, holding out a hand. "And your handcuffs."

The Sheriff yanked the keys from his pocket, tearing the pocket in his haste. He continued to shake and sob.

"Now where are your handcuffs?"

"Other pocket. Here they are." Banjo Billy ripped his other pocket in his haste to produce the cuffs. Max snapped them over Banjo Billy's wrists. Then Max pulled a length of twine from his pocket and wrapped it around Banjo Billy's legs. He tied the Sheriff's ankles together.

"You won't be able to strut for awhile," he told the Sheriff. "Or swagger."

Banjo Bill grunted.

"I'm going to lock you in this room, Billy. This bad old bear will be right outside the door. Don't make a move or I'll sic him on you."

From inside the head of the bear came a growl that was so realistic Max almost laughed.

"Not a peep. Keep him away from me," the Sheriff squealed.

"One more thing," Max growled. "You'd be wise not to tell anyone about this, unless you want to be the butt of a lot of jokes from the Bradley brothers."

"Of course. I won't tell. Not a peep," the Sheriff said, his voice cracking. "I'm not stupid."

"Oh, you'll tell all right," Max said gruffly. "But not for awhile."

From another pocket, Max pulled some cloth and wrapped it around Billy's head, sealing his lips but making sure he could still breathe through his nose.

"You'll be back to your arrogance and bullying in good time—as soon as someone finds you," Max said. "Maybe you should give some thought to changing your ways."

Max locked the door to the room and walked quickly over to the cell. He opened the cell door and motioned for Susan and Marty to come out.

"Gee, is that you, Max? You scared us half to death," Marty whispered, grinning. "Then that must be Sammy," he said, reaching out to pat the bear's head.

Sammy snarled, showing his yellow teeth, and Marty jumped a foot in the air.

"Yikes!" he cried.

"Who are those two sleeping beauties?" Max asked, nodding toward Mort and Lefty.

"Tell you later," Marty said.

"I can't wait," Max said curtly. "You okay, Susan?"

"My leg hurts where I kicked that awful man," she said, smiling. "But I'm sure he hurts more."

"Good. Let's get out of here."

They started for the door when Marty grabbed Max by the elbow.

"Wait a minute," said Marty.

"What is it?"

"I've got to untie some shoelaces. Only be a minute."

Moments later, the four teenagers slipped out the door and closed it behind them. Just then, Max looked up the street and saw the Bradley brothers huddled on the corner.

"Time to call it a night," he heard Bart say to Hugo.

"Wait a minute," Hugo replied. "It's odd we didn't see Banjo Billy tonight. He probably fell asleep in that old rocking chair again. I'd better go check on him."

Bart turned and walked away while Hugo, his head down, sauntered along the street leading to the jail. He was less than 100 yards away.

"Quick! Slip around the corner of the building," Max whispered. "And stay in the shadows. We've got to get back to the car."

The four teenagers moved silently around the corner and then broke into a run, retracing their steps to the DeSoto.

A few minutes later, somewhere behind them, they heard Hugo's voice.

"Help! Help! There's been a jailbreak!"

Sammy, meanwhile, was pleading with his car.

"Sweetheart, be good to me," he begged. "Be my baby. Don't be cranky tonight."

"Who in the world are you talking to?" Max asked, breathing hard.

"The DeSoto," Sammy answered. "She may be mad at me for leaving her alone in this awful town. Mad enough that she may not start."

But the DeSoto was neither angry with Sammy nor concerned about her surroundings. She purred like a pussycat when Sammy turned the key, then moved quietly down the streets that led to the main road. And a few minutes later, she brought them safely back to the village.

CHAPTER 17

THE SHOWDOWN

It was Saturday morning. All around Tumbling Waters, people were packing up, getting ready to leave. In groups, at breakfast and afterwards, they met with Chief Echo to thank him for his hospitality. The powwow had been a great success, despite the burning of the longhouse and the interference of the Bradleys. The various tribes promised to meet again the following summer.

"The main road has been repaired. You can drive out that way," the Chief suggested.

"No, we enjoyed the drive in over the logging trails your people cleared for us," the other chiefs said. "We will leave by those routes and not have to pass through Silver City."

"Too bad," Sammy interjected. "That means you'll miss giving the Bradley gang lots of goodbye hugs and kisses."

"Just the thought of that makes me ill," Chief

Whitecoat of the Ottawas said, turning to spit in the grass, demonstrating how he felt about the Bradleys. "Chief Echo," he said, shaking hands. "Good luck to you in your dispute with them. Remember what our people have learned in 500 years. White men cannot be trusted."

"Well, some of them can," the Chief replied, nodding toward Max and Marty.

"Yes, you are right. They are fine young men," Chief Whitecoat agreed. He walked over to Max. "I admire you, young man, for helping your brother and Susan get out of jail. What you did was illegal, of course, and the Sheriff will be very angry. Perhaps he'll arrest you next. But brothers must look out for each other. That bumbling Sheriff was wrong to put innocent teenagers in jail."

"I thought Banjo Billy might show up here today, looking for Susan and Marty. And Max and Sammy, too," Chief Echo said. "If he does, I can honestly say I have not seen them lately." He pulled some dark glasses from his pocket and put them on. "I will wear these. It's hard to see anyone with these glasses on."

But the Sheriff didn't show up.

The visitors left.

Chief Echo entered the longhouse and emerged moments later wearing his ceremonial garb. It was almost time to meet with the Bradleys.

The tribal members gathered at the centre of a meadow.

The Bradleys arrived in force. Most of the residents of Silver City had been recruited to attend the meeting. Almost all had guns—revolvers mostly and a couple of shotguns. They outnumbered the Indian delegation by two or three to one.

Blackjack Bradley was in the lead, flanked by his wife Myrtle and his sons Bart and Hugo. Banjo Billy the Sheriff trailed behind. Apparently, on this day, he preferred to keep a low profile, still feeling humiliated by the events of the night before. When Hugo Bradley had found him handcuffed in his rocking chair, he had laughed. "By gum, Billy, them kids musta thrown a real scare at you. I do believe you've peed your pants."

The two groups approached each other, like two armies about to collide on a battlefield. They stopped about ten yards apart.

Blackjack Bradley was the first to speak.

"Hey, Chief," he called out jovially. "How about it? Have you made up your mind about my offer?"

"Let's talk about this land first," Chief Echo replied, waving his hand at the trees and rocky outcroppings that surrounded them. "You say you have a deed to it, and I say our band has a deed to it. May I see your deed once more?"

Blackjack Bradley fished in his pocket and pulled out his deed. He handed it to the Chief, who examined it closely.

"Mr. Bradley, the date on this deed is the exact same date as the date on ours. Is that not unusual?"

"Just coincidence, Chief."

"But ours was filed many, many years ago."

"That so? Well, so was mine, Chief."

"Mr. Bradley, I have been alive many more years than you. If you filed this yourself, you must have been in kindergarten. You must have been only three years or four years old. I find it odd that a three-year-old would file a land deed."

Bradley had never noticed the date on the deed. For a moment, he was speechless. But he recovered quickly. Boldly, he stated, "The date's not the important thing, Chief, the signature is. And that's my signature."

"Is it? Well, it's a fine signature—for a three-year-old," answered the Chief. There was a ripple of laughter from some of the townsfolk, until Bart and Hugo Bradley turned and glared at them.

"Furthermore," said the Chief, "both signatures, yours and mine, appear to be smudged, mine because someone spat on it and yours because, well, perhaps you can explain it to me."

The Chief looked up into a face that was quickly growing redder than any of his tribe members. Red with anger.

"Are you suggesting that I tampered with this deed, smudging my name?" Bradley shouted. Just then, his wife Myrtle stepped forward. "Dear, I brought a copy of the deed with me," she said, handing a document to her husband. "Your signature is a little clearer on this one."

Blackjack looked at the paper and said, "My, my, so it is," and handed it triumphantly to Chief Echo.

"Thank you, Mrs. Bradley," the Chief said, nodding politely in her direction. He smiled and asked, "But why would you have two copies of the deed? A second copy is always kept in the deeds office in Capital City. A clerk there stamps it and files it. Is that not right, Mrs. Bradley? I believe you worked there at one time." He looked more closely at the document. "Say, this is interesting. There's a government stamp on this second deed. Can you tell me how you got this deed, Mrs. Bradley?"

A look of guilt swept across her face. "Well, I... I... the thing is..."

Myrtle Bradley was unable to speak. But her husband could.

Blackjack Bradley caught her look and stepped close to the Chief. He went on the attack.

"Are you calling my wife a thief? A forger?" snarled Bradley, "Because if you are, you'll regret it."

"That's right," echoed his two sons, making a show of handling the guns on their hips.

"I called her neither one," the Chief insisted, his voice steady. "I merely asked her a question."

Blackjack Bradley stepped back. "Listen, Chief, we're never going to settle this matter to anyone's satisfaction unless we hire lawyers and spend a fortune on them. Tell you what, why not settle it with a competition—my men against yours?"

"You mean a fight, a battle?" the Chief said, puzzled by the remark.

"No, I mean a contest," Blackjack Bradley said. "You Indians are wonderful shooters with your bows and arrows. My men have guns. Let's set up a few targets and we'll fire away—you with your arrows, we with our bullets. The winner gets the land, the loser tears up his deed."

"We don't use bows and arrows the way we once did," Chief Echo said. "Mostly guns now—when we hunt. We would be at a disadvantage in such a contest."

"Come on, Chief. You had a contest just the other day. I heard there was some superb archery."

Chief Echo sighed. He thought, *What trick does Blackjack Bradley have up his sleeve now? I am weary of this dispute. I wish the Bradleys would go away and stay away. Or perhaps it's better if my people go away. Some distance between us would be a good thing.*

"Hmm. Bullets against arrows," he mused, repeating Bradley's words. "From what distance will we shoot?" he asked.

"Let's say 100 yards."

"That's much too far for accuracy with a bow and arrow—25 yards is better."

"Heck, that's child's play," Blackjack scoffed. "How about 75 yards?"

"Make it 75 yards for you and 25 yards for us," said the Chief. "I told you, we don't use bows and arrows much anymore. We do it to maintain one of our traditions."

"Make it 40 yards for your archers," Bradley stated.

"Still too far," the Chief replied. "How about 30 yards for us?"

He thought, *Bradley will be surprised at the accuracy of our archers from 30 yards. His shooters, using their pistols, will be hard pressed to hit small targets from 75 yards.* He smelled an advantage, even though his instincts told him not to trust the Bradleys.

"Done!" said Blackjack. "We'll put some targets up on those two trees over there. You pick three of your best archers and I'll pick three of my best shots. The Sheriff has some paper targets. He'll nail yours to the tree on the left and mine to the tree next to it. This will be fun, because the bull's eye in the targets is only four inches in diameter."

The Sheriff ran off to place the targets. Then he began to pace off 75 yards, using tiny baby steps as a measure.

"No, no, no!" shouted Chief Echo angrily. "Billy is

making one yard out of two. We will use Maude Greentree's tape measure in place of Billy's small feet. Someone run and get it."

Someone did, and ten minutes later both distances had been measured accurately.

A coin was flipped to see who would shoot first, and Blackjack won the toss.

"My two sons, Bart and Hugo, will be my shooters—along with myself," he declared.

Chief Echo looked around. He said, "I will select Elmo Swift, Susan Greentree and Max Mitchell."

Hugo Bradley laughed out loud. "Hey, Pop, he picked one crazy Indian, one outsider and a little girl," he scoffed. "Surely you can do better than that, Chief."

"I stand by my choices," said the Chief, giving Hugo a withering look. "Go ahead. Shoot your pistol."

But Hugo just laughed and put his pistol down. Myrtle Bradley stepped forward, a smirk on her face, and handed Hugo a blanket. He unrolled it and brought forth a shiny new rifle—an expensive one.

"Who said anything about pistols?" he said, still chuckling. "My dad said we'd use bullets against your arrows. Didn't mention pistols, did he? Since rifles are more accurate than pistols, I'm going to use this one."

"But that's not fair," Maude Greentree shouted in

anger. "We assumed you were going to use pistols. That's what you're all carrying."

Chief Echo raised his hand. "It's all right, Maude. Hugo is right. I did say bullets. Nothing about the guns that shoot them. We'll have to live up to the terms of the wager."

Banjo Billy broke into a grin so wide he almost split his lip. "And here's another surprise," he said, moving forward and handing Hugo a cylinder-shaped device. Hugo immediately began attaching it to his rifle.

"What's that thing?" Sammy asked.

"Why, it's a new telescopic sight," Hugo answered, sneering at Sammy. "The old Chief forgot to mention scopes weren't allowed when the bet was made, either. Oh boy, that was dumb."

The Chief threw up his arms. No wonder Blackjack Bradley accepted the 75-yard distance without much argument. Pistols would have been useless from that range. He realized the Bradleys now had all the advantage. He turned to his people and said bitterly. "I'm very sorry, my friends. I made a big mistake. It's a terrible wager."

"Aw, don't worry about it, Chief," someone said. "This land is not all that valuable, anyway. Even less now that they've killed all the fish."

Marty groaned. "No way bows and arrows can beat rifles with telescopes!" he said.

"Telescopic sights," corrected Max. "And don't be too sure. We may have been conned but we're not going to concede. This contest isn't over." He gave Marty a weak grin. "Not by a long shot."

CHAPTER 18
ARCHERS VERSUS GUNMEN

Hugo Bradley was already standing behind the line drawn in the dirt. Seventy-five yards had been measured from the tree to the line and he was anxious to use the new rifle with the telescopic sight.

"Wait!" cried the Chief. "I appoint myself one of the referees. I will stand by the tree and check the targets. One of your men can do the same, Mr. Bradley."

"Okay by me," Blackjack said. "Banjo Billy, you stay up there and check out the hits and misses."

The brief delay had made Hugo edgy. He was anxious to shoot, perhaps too anxious. He pulled the trigger.

Baaannnng! The bullet slammed through the target and went deep into the trunk of the tree. But it missed the bull's eye by a fraction.

"Curses!" shouted Hugo, shaking the rifle as if it were the carbine's fault.

Elmo Swift took his place behind the 30-yard line

and carefully laid down his crutch. Stony-faced, he took a moment to glare at the Bradleys.

Noting the malice in Elmo's look, Bart muttered, "What did we do to him?" muttered Bart.

Elmo was calm and confident, collecting his balance on his one good leg. He drew back the bowstring, took careful aim and the arrow whistled through the air, plunking into the target but an inch shy of the bull's eye.

His supporters groaned. Dismayed, Elmo shook his head, picked up his crutch and backed away.

The next shooter was Bart Bradley. He took the prized rifle from his brother and grumbled, "Some shooter you turned out to be, Hugo. Couldn't hit the bull's eye even with the new telescopic sight."

"Aw, quit mouthin' off. Let's see you do any better."

Bart took his time shouldering the rifle. Then he aimed and fired.

"Bull's eye!" yelled the Sheriff, jumping up and down in joy and clapping his hands.

The Bradley gang whooped and hollered and Bart threw the rifle high in the air, catching it with one hand when it descended.

"Wait a minute!" shouted Chief Echo, moving in to examine the target. "That was close but it was no bull's eye," he called out. "The Sheriff needs glasses. Come see for yourself, Mr. Bradley."

Blackjack Bradley ran toward the target and was

forced to admit that the Chief was right. Bart's bullet had missed the edge of the bull's eye by the width of a feather.

Blackjack gave Banjo Billy a withering look and clipped him on the back of the neck with a big hand, knocking his hat off. The Sheriff threw up his hands and muttered, "Hey, I tried, boss. I didn't think that old man's eyes were very good. I figured he'd never notice the shot missed."

Back behind the shooter's line, Max and Susan put their heads together. "You shoot last, Max," Susan said. "I'm a little nervous."

"No, Susan," Max replied firmly. "You proved you're the best archer in camp. You proved you couldn't be rattled. I have a hunch it'll come down to last shot. Lend me your bow. I'll shoot next."

Max stood behind the line. He raised the bow and took a deep breath. At 30 yards, the target seemed to be a mile away.

He released the arrow and heard the *thrumm* of its flight as it sped away. It smacked into the target and Max held his breath as the Sheriff and Chief Echo examined the hole it made.

"Bull's eye!" shouted the Chief, stepping back and smiling at Max. He gave him a thumbs-up. Banjo Billy smacked a fist into the trunk of the tree and cried out in pain. "Dern it, that hurt," he said with a grimace. Still angry, he kicked a rotten log with his boot. The rot in the log flew up and some of it struck him in his face. There were ants in the rot and they crawled down his shirt and into his hair. He danced around, slapping at his head and chest while everyone roared with laughter.

"Arrest those ants, Billy," someone called out. "And their uncles, too. Put yer handcuffs on them. Charge them with assault!"

Finally, things settled down and it was Blackjack's turn to shoot. He paused to say to his two sons, "You boys guaranteed me the rifle with the scope would win this wager," he muttered angrily. "Do I have to do everything myself?"

He shouldered the rifle and took his place. Blackjack was an expert shooter. Some people said he could shoot a toothpick out of a man's mouth from 50 paces, but nobody had ever seen him do it. Even in Silver City, where slow-witted men were in the majority, nobody had been willing to let him try. But he had an eye with a rifle. He was the kind of sharpshooter who could put a bullet through the knothole in a fence from 100 yards.

Blackjack waved to the crowd, calmly took aim and punctured the heart of the target with a brilliant shot. Bull's eye!

The competition was tied and there was one shooter left: Susan Greentree.

"Thank goodness, it's just a girl shooting against

us," Bart Bradley said to his brother. "Girls can't shoot. Not guns, not arrows. Maybe a slingshot, but even that's a stretch... ha, ha! Looks like we're the new landowners here."

Hugo agreed. He spat in the dirt and chortled. "The old Chief better step aside. She may shoot an arrow through his foot."

"Yeah. Or somewhere else," laughed Bart.

"Shut up, you two," their father ordered. "This isn't over yet."

Susan's face was impassive as she notched the arrow in her bow. If she was nervous, it did not show. She stood at the line and never wavered. The arrow fled from her bow and flew straight at the target. But would it hit dead centre?

Whump!

Chief Echo knew immediately that it was a bull's eye. He hollered, "Great shot, Susan! Great shot!"

The Indians surged forward and pounded Susan on the back. They embraced her and shook her hand. Max and Marty hoisted her on their shoulders and walked her around in circles.

Suddenly, the noisy celebration came to a halt. A car horn was beeping madly and its noise caused everyone to turn in the direction of the main road.

The car swerved off the highway and turned into the field on which the two rival groups stood. Dust flew up from the car's fenders as it bounced over the ground and came skidding to a halt.

"Hey, that's Dad's car," Marty yelped.

"Yep. And Mom's in it with some other folks," Max said, as he and Sammy lowered Susan to the ground.

Mr. and Mrs. Mitchell got out of the car, while two strangers wearing business suits emerged from the back seat.

Amy Mitchell came straight to Max and Marty and draped her arms over their shoulders. She would have kissed her sons, but she surmised that, under the circumstances, it might have embarrassed them. Meanwhile, Harry Mitchell huddled briefly with Chief Echo. Then, he addressed the crowd.

"Ladies and gentlemen, my name is Harry Mitchell and I'm the owner and editor of the *Indian River Review*. I understand from Chief Echo that you have just settled a land dispute by means of a shooting contest.

"Well, I'm here to tell you that if the result had gone the other way, that if Mr. Bradley and his boys had won, there would have been an even bigger contest—probably in a court of law. You see, the two distinguished gentleman who've joined me here today are from Capital City. They're both government men and both are lawyers. Mr. Lyall Mason over here is in law enforcement. The other gentleman is a member of the Iroquois tribe—George Littlewood."

"So what's that got to do with us?" Hugo Bradley asked rudely.

"Well, it seems you Bradleys have been engaging in some questionable activities in Silver City," Harry Mitchell said.

"Like what?" shouted Bart Bradley.

"Like trying to cheat Chief Echo out of this land that he rightfully bought for his people," Harry Mitchell replied. "That deed Blackjack Bradley carries is a fake. Don't believe me? Ask Mr. Mason, who's just finished a complete investigation. He's here to ask Myrtle Bradley how the deed disappeared from the deeds office files."

"You'll have trouble proving anything," Blackjack Bradley said calmly.

"Perhaps. Perhaps not," said Harry Mitchell. "But there are other reasons for us to be here. Could I speak with your Sheriff, please?"

"That's Banjo Billy. He's hiding over there, behind that tree," one of the folks from town said. "He's got ants in his pants."

"Mr. Billy, come forward, please. Why are you hiding?"

"I was not hiding. I was looking for acorns," Banjo Billy said indignantly.

"If you'll look closely, Mr. Billy, you'll note that's a maple tree. Oak trees leave acorns."

"Well, I'll be derned, so it is," Banjo Billy said, scratching at his neck.

"Mr. Billy, I understand you're the Sheriff in these parts."

"That's right."

"And you put two young people in your jail last night?"

"I sure did—for verbally assaulting a police officer. And then they escaped. They used a bear to help them get away. Say, you can call me Banjo Billy. Everybody else does."

George Littlewood stepped forward. "I remember you from when I was a child on the reserve, Banjo Billy. You used to shoot rats at the dump with your BB gun. You were a mean little so-and-so then. Haven't changed much, have you? How'd you get to be sheriff?"

Banjo Billy was surprised by the question. "What's that?" he said.

"Were you elected? Appointed? How'd you become sheriff? It's a simple question, Billy."

Banjo Billy gulped. He looked around as if hoping someone would answer for him. Finally he said, "I was appointed, I guess."

"And who appointed you to be the gun-toting saviour of Silver City?" George Littlewood said pleasantly.

"Why, well, it was... it was... it was Blackjack Bradley, that's who."

"Did Mr. Bradley have the authority to make such an appointment?" George Littlewood asked.

"Well, heck, I don't know," Banjo Billy answered. "He just done it."

Lyall Mason turned to Blackjack Bradley.

"Well, Mr. Bradley? Do you have the authority to appoint the sheriff of Silver City?"

"Sure I do. I'm the Mayor here, ain't I?"

"The Mayor? Did you win the last election for mayor by a large majority?"

"Sure, I did. Almost everybody in town voted for me."

"And when was that election, Mr. Bradley?"

Blackjack looked skyward for a minute, and then said, "Oh, about a dozen years ago."

"Twelve years, Mr. Bradley. Don't you understand that elections are to be held every four years? Why didn't you call for elections, Mr. Bradley?"

"I'm a busy man, sir," Blackjack replied. "Got a mine to run. Besides, I forgot."

People began to laugh. "Old Blackjack's in a pickle now," one of them hooted. "He forgot to call elections. And nobody pushed him to because almost everybody in town works for him."

"He didn't forget," Lyall Mason told the crowd. "Every four years, he reported the election results to the government: 'Bradley wins in another land-slide.'"

Harry Mitchell pulled a newspaper from his pocket. He unfolded it and held it up.

"Folks, this is the headline I'm running in the next edition of the *Indian River Review*. It reads:

Blackjack Bradley Charged by Government Investigators. Sheriff of Silver City Found to be a Fraud. Charged with Illegal Arrest of Teens. Hugo and Bart Bradley Charged with Illegal Use of Dynamite and Arson in Burning of Iroquois Longhouse.

"Those are serious charges," Harry Mitchell added. "Are there any others, gentlemen?"

George Littlewood raised his hand. "Yes, there's another charge of fraud pending against Mr. Bradley, for selling logging rights that don't belong to him."

"Really?" said Harry Mitchell, as if that were news to him.

"Yes, it appears Mr. Bradley was willing to swap the reserve land set aside for Chief Echo and his people for a tract of land about ten miles from here. But Mr. Bradley doesn't own that land, the government does. If Mr. Bradley has a deed to that land, it's a fake. What's more, Mr. Bradley sold the logging rights to that land to a man named Prendergast. I called Prendergast today and he's furious. Wants his down payment back immediately."

Chief Echo wanted to speak. "Gentlemen, I hear you saying that if I had accepted Mr. Bradley's deal and moved to that land ten miles from here, some-day Mr. Prendergast would come along and begin chopping all the trees down. That was terribly dishonest, Mr. Bradley, very fraudulent."

"To say the least," added Harry Mitchell.

"Besides," Mr. Mason said, "If you want that land ten miles from here—and I understand it's in a beautiful valley—George Littlewood and I will see that you get it for free. I'm sure the government would agree to a relocation of your reserve."

"There's great fishing up there," Sammy shouted. "The lake is full of fish—and they're not dead, either."

"Then we shall move there," said Chief Echo. "And we shall decide later what to do with this land." The Indians applauded their Chief's decision.

"Come on, let's get out of here," Blackjack Bradley said, somewhat stunned by the turn of events. He turned and led his followers to a grove of trees, where they sat down to discuss their predicament. Some of the townspeople who had accompanied him to the showdown kept walking, headed for home. They were fed up with the control the Bradleys had held over them.

"We've got to go, too," Harry Mitchell said. "I've got to get these fine gentlemen back to Capital City. Then it's back to the office to work on the paper. I guess we'll see you boys next week."

Chief Echo thanked Harry Mitchell and his friends for their help and, always the gentleman, took Amy Mitchell by the arm and assisted her into the car. He turned to embrace George Littlewood and told him how proud he was that a member of the Iroquois community had done so well in life.

"We need more like you, George," he said.

When his father moved behind the wheel, Max stuck his head in the car window and said, "Dad, one question."

"What is it, son?"

"Were you really going to print that headline you read out to the Bradleys?"

"Heck, no, son. I had to come here and get more information. But now that I've got it, I'll print one that's very similar. And I'd like you to work on the body of the story."

Max grinned. "I can do that," he said.

CHAPTER 19
A FINAL CONFRONTATION

Blackjack Bradley sat in the deep grass and stared at the ground. He was in a foul mood. He and his sons had been outshot by three kids with bows and arrows. His counterfeit deeds to the property had been exposed by that newspaperman, Harry Mitchell. He was in big trouble now and he knew it. And so were his wife and those lazy sons of his.

He looked up and saw Chief Echo and his tribe lingering in the field. They were still chatting about the events of the day, no doubt chuckling over how they'd outsmarted the Bradley clan. A wave of anger rushed over him.

Blackjack called Banjo Billy over. "How many men have we got—men with guns?" he asked.

Billy made a count. "About 30," he said.

"And how many of the Indians are still in the field?"

"I'd guess about 12, maybe 15," said Billy, cupping a hand over his eyes.

"Want to teach those Indians a lesson? Put a real scare into them?" Blackjack asked, rising to his feet. "For humiliating us?"

"I sure do," said Billy.

"Those Mitchell kids deserve a good beating just for siding with the Indians," Blackjack snarled.

Hugo was excited at the thought of beating up on Max. He figured Max was 20 pounds lighter and two inches shorter. And four or five years younger. Hugo was a bully and seldom challenged anyone his own size.

"Let's go get 'em," said brother Bart. "At least we'll scare the britches off them. Maybe we can even burn down their new longhouse."

Blackjack assembled his men and told them to load their guns. "When we chase them, use the shotguns," he barked. "But shoot over their heads. We want to scare them, not actually shoot anyone."

The Bradley gang walked briskly toward the Chief and his people, guns upraised. Hugo pulled the trigger of his shotgun and a shot whistled over the head of Chief Echo. The Chief and his followers were startled.

"Run for the reserve!" shouted the Chief.

"Susan," said Max. "You run on ahead. We don't want you to get hurt."

"No, they're just trying to scare us," Susan said stubbornly. "I'm staying with my friends."

Another blast sent pellets flying overhead. Then another.

"Run for it!" Chief Echo ordered. "Run for the longhouse."

The group ran swiftly over the rough ground. Another 100 yards and they would be over the boundary of the reserve and into the trees. Surely the Bradleys wouldn't chase them in there. But some of the Bradley gang members were scooting across the field at an angle, attempting to get ahead of the Indians. They were trying to cut off their escape route.

More shots and more pellets flew overhead, but a little lower this time.

Hugo Bradley got caught up in the excitement of the chase. He raised his shotgun and fired. But just as he pulled the trigger, he stumbled over a small rock and was thrown off stride. The gun barrel dropped and the shot flew straight at Elmo Swift, who had thrown down his crutch and was hobbling across the ground with surprising speed. Elmo screamed and fell, dropping his bow. His quiver of arrows flew off his back and blood quickly stained his shirt. Elmo rolled on the ground, groaning in pain.

Max raced over to assist Elmo. He tore the bloodied shirt aside and saw a couple of pellet holes in Elmo's back.

"Are you okay, Elmo?" Max asked.

"Yes, more surprised than anything. He just nicked me with some buckshot. Max, look out! Hugo Bradley is coming fast. Looks like he's planning to shoot you next."

Max dove through the grass and found Elmo's bow. He notched an arrow in it and swung around to see Hugo Bradley closing in, his shotgun raised. *Hugo's gone berserk*, Max thought. *He really intends to shoot me.*

Max rose to one knee, took aim and fired an arrow straight at Hugo Bradley's raised arm. The sharp arrowhead struck the shotgun and it flew from Hugo's hands, spinning high in the air and falling into the deep grass.

Hugo snarled and plunged through the grass at Max. Max had just enough time to get to his feet and brace himself when Hugo piled into him.

"You traitor," Hugo growled. "Running around with reserve friends. I'm going to give you the whipping of your life."

Hugo Bradley weighed well over 200 pounds, but much of it was fat. When he moved in close, he took a wild punch at Max. Max ducked and drove his fist into the man's stomach. When he heard a loud "Ooomph!" he drove a second fist into the same spot. There was another "Ooomph!" Hugo doubled over, gasping for breath. He managed to grab Max by the arms and he hung on while he fought to regain his breath. Max struggled to break free but Hugo had wrists of steel. Hugo made a quick recovery from the blows to the stomach and laughed out loud.

"Now I'm going to break all your ribs," he threatened, encircling Max with a powerful bear hug. Max was lifted off his feet. He pounded on Hugo's back but he couldn't break the bear hug. Dust and grass flew in all directions as they struggled. Max was rapidly losing his breath—and his strength. His father had always told him to fight fair. On the hockey rink, on the baseball field, he was known for his sportsmanship. But this was serious. In a moment or two he'd be unconscious and Hugo Bradley would be kicking at his ribs.

Max struggled for balance, and then quickly brought his right knee up between Hugo's legs. Hugo howled in pain and partially released his grip. Max took a deep breath, and then placed his right leg behind Hugo's left. He pushed hard and Hugo flew over backwards, landing heavily on his back. Max leaped on him and put a headlock around Hugo's neck. But Hugo was finished. He had no stamina and was winded by the fall. And the grip Max held him in was choking him.

"You quit, Hugo?" Max asked him. "Had enough?"

"Yeah, I quit. Lemme up."

"What's the magic word, Hugo?"

"The magic word? Oh, you mean 'Please?'"

"That's right, Hugo. Please let me up, Max. Say it!"

"Okay. *Please* let me up, Max."

Max released his hold and Hugo rose slowly to his feet.

"Now go and apologize to Elmo," Max demanded. "You could have killed him."

Humiliated, Hugo staggered over to Elmo, whose wounds were being attended to by Susan and Marty. Stoney and Maude Greentree rushed over and helped lift Elmo to his feet. They started walking him in the direction of the longhouse.

"Elmo, I'm real sorry," whimpered Hugo, trailing behind. "We were trying to scare you all, not shoot you. I stumbled and my gun went off. I'm sorry, Elmo."

"I'll survive, so I guess I can accept your apology," Elmo murmured.

"Look! Over there!" Max shouted. The tribe members, led by Chief Echo, were now some distance away. And the fast-moving Bradley gang had cut off their escape to the longhouse. They were surrounded and things were getting ugly.

"Marty, come with me!" Max ordered. "We've got to go help the Chief."

Max, Marty and Susan raced across the field to where the Chief and his men were surrounded. "Blackjack and his bullies are about to explode," Max shouted.

"Indians like to dance," they heard Blackjack Bradley cry out. "Then dance."

Bradley pulled out a pistol and pumped bullets into the dirt at the feet of the Chief. The shots kicked up dirt within inches of his moccasins. Chief Echo looked back defiantly and refused to move his feet. "I'll shoot your toes off, Chief, if you don't dance," Blackjack threatened.

"Go ahead," the Chief answered, scornfully. "I will not dance for you. I will not be bullied by your kind."

Blackjack raised his pistol and was pointing it at the Chief's feet when he noticed movement in the trees some distance away. The parting of branches distracted him.

From the trees emerged at least 200 Indians, all carrying bows and arrows. They stood in a long row and lifted their bows. And their arrows were pointed directly at him.

"What the..." Blackjack Bradley couldn't believe he was facing such a well-armed force. There was no doubt they were ready to attack. He felt light-headed. He began to perspire, his hands began to tremble and he thought he might faint. Hundreds of arrows were pointed at his chest. "Who are those people?" he mumbled. He'd never been so afraid in his life.

The Chief smiled and waved at the row of Indians. "They are my cousins. They were here for the powwow."

"But they went home early this morning," Blackjack stammered.

"I did not trust you, so I asked that they remain hidden. Just in case. It is what people in your world call... *insurance.*"

Blackjack Bradley panicked. His group was vastly outnumbered. And he'd just witnessed how accurate Indians could be with their deadly arrows.

"Don't shoot," he shouted, raising both arms. He knew he was whipped. "We were just leaving." He glared at Chief Echo accusingly. "You told me you didn't use bows and arrows much anymore."

"Did I?" Chief Echo responded. "Perhaps I'm just as surprised as you are. Now why don't you drop your weapons and leave."

As he trudged off, head down in defeat, Blackjack brushed past Max and Susan. He couldn't resist roughly nudging Susan with his elbow. "Watch it, squaw!" he growled as he stormed across the meadow.

On silent feet, she ran after him and delivered a kick that knocked him to his knees. Before she could deliver another kick, Blackjack scuttled away. Susan came back, her face still red with anger.

"Give me that bow and get me an arrow," she said to Max.

"Susan, you can't shoot him in the back," Max protested.

"Oh, I know that, silly. I'll just shoot an arrow

over his head. It'll make him move a little faster."

Her shot whistled over the head of Blackjack Bradley and he jumped like a startled rabbit. The villagers dissolved into helpless peels of laughter watching him scamper away.

"He runs fast, like Tom Longboat," observed the Chief, his eyes twinkling.

Susan's arrow struck a rocky outcropping. The arrowhead sent a chip of rock flying.

The teenagers turned to find Chief Echo mingling with his cousins. Their eyes were wet from laughing.

"What's so funny?" Max asked.

"You saw all those bows and arrows aimed at the Bradley men?" the Chief answered, still chuckling.

"Yes, I saw them. They scared the heck out of that mob."

"Look at this," said the Chief, handing Max one of the bows. Max saw immediately that it wasn't a bow at all, not a real one, and he began to laugh. It was just a bow-sized tree branch stripped of its bark. And the arrows were just as phony, smaller branches stripped of their covering. "Why, they're just as counterfeit as the Bradley land deeds." Max said, still chuckling.

"We brought a few bows and arrows to the powwow," one of the elders said. "But not enough to scare anybody. So we improvised."

"From a distance, they looked like bows and

arrows to me," Marty said. "Hundreds of them. No wonder the Bradleys scuttled away. But what if they'd caught on that you had no weapons—no real ones?"

"Then I guess we'd have stuck our tongues out at them—before we turned and ran like Longboat," Chief Whitecoat of the Ottawas said, drawing still more laughter.

"Let's get back to the reserve and celebrate our victory," someone said.

"You celebrate. We must go," Chief Whitecoat said. "We are hours behind schedule, but it was worth our while to wait. What fun we had! For a few minutes it was like playing cowboys and Indians."

"We can't thank you enough," Chief Echo said, embracing the other chiefs.

"We must stick together—our people," said Chief Whitecoat quietly. "It will remain that way for a long time to come."

After his friends had slipped silently into the woods again, Chief Echo led his followers back to the longhouse.

"That arrow you shot over Blackjack's head frightened him so much I thought he was going to... well, never mind what I thought," Marty said to Susan and Max. "Let's go fetch the arrow for a souvenir." They ran through the field until they found the spot where the arrow landed, and Marty picked it up. He handed it to Susan.

"You keep it, Marty," she said. "Hang it in your bedroom at home. When you look at it from time to time, think of the many friends you've made in the past few days."

Marty beamed and said, "I will. That's a great idea. Thank you, Susan."

"Hey, here's where it hit the boulder," Max said, reaching down to pick up the chip of rock that the sharp arrowhead had dislodged. He stared at it curiously, then reached in his pocket and pulled out the small rock that he had "borrowed" from Marty's collection.

"There's something strange here," he said, turning the two rock chips over in his hand. "I want Chief Echo to see these."

Back in the longhouse, Chief Echo examined the rock chips. He paused for several seconds, his face impassive.

"What is it, Chief?" Marty asked. "You have a strange look on your face."

"I believe you young people have made a rare discovery," the Chief answered. "Inside both rocks, I see streaks of silver. It's possible you have discovered a vein of silver on this property. No wonder Blackjack Bradley wanted this land so badly. He must have suspected there was more silver in this area. That arrow you shot, Susan, may mean that we will become very rich."

The Chief smiled broadly. "If there happens to be another silver mine under the ground we walk on, and if it makes us wealthy, we shall share the wealth with all our cousins and keep very little for ourselves." He winked at Marty. "But enough to replace the old DeSoto. And build some houses with real lumber."

"And if the vein of the silver mine—if there is one—leads to the ground under your longhouse, what then, Chief?" Max asked.

"We shall move, of course—to that land ten miles from here. In fact, we shall do that anyway. Remember, we have been taught to respect the land we live on. We would be foolish to allow miners with their heavy equipment and their crude behaviour anywhere near where we live. There is an old saying in our culture: 'If you dig precious things from the land, you may be inviting disaster.'"

The old Chief sighed and turned to Max.

"You have lived among us for a little while—you and Marty. Perhaps now you understand how we feel. We are not that different from our ancestors. They did not invite the white men to come here to North America. We have always believed that the Great Spirit gave us this country as a home. The white men who came here—the Spaniards, the French, the English—all had their own land across the ocean. Did we interfere with them? No. Were we hostile toward them? No. Did we jump in our canoes and cross the ocean and push them from their land? No. The Great Spirit gave us plenty of land to live on, and plenty of buffalo, deer, antelope and other game. And enough fish for all. But the white man came here and shot our game and caught our fish, until there was very little left for us or for anybody else. For almost a hundred years, it has been very difficult for us to live as we once did. We shall never enjoy that kind of life again."

CHAPTER 20

TIME TO GO HOME

Chief Echo called the young people to his longhouse and asked them to sit. Susan and Sammy were there, along with Max and Marty. Then Elmo Swift entered, flashed a quick smile and sat down too.

"Before I speak, do you have any questions?" the Chief asked.

"Will it bother you to move to a new reserve, Chief Echo?" Max asked.

"No, my son, it will cause no distress," answered the Chief. "Our people have been on the move for a long time, pushed here and there by white men. Often, the treaties they signed with us proved worthless. The white man broke hundreds of them over the years. If they wanted to build a big dam for electricity, they built it, even though it flooded our ancestral homes. If they wanted to bulldoze a road through our reserves, they found a way to do it. Treaties were brushed aside, like bugs off a windowsill. One of my cousins, Cora Baker, once wrote that her people were forced out of their valley much like gophers—once water is poured on gopher holes, they can either leave or drown. That's how it was. Can you imagine? And a man named Beacham once wrote that Indians being cheated by the government was nothing to worry about, because, in his eyes, we were just Indians, of no value."

"Well, we think it's wrong. And it's been wrong for a very long time," Max stated.

"The Pawnee people had a saying: 'What is past and cannot be prevented should not be grieved for,'" the Chief said with a sigh.

"Chief, we had a really good time at your pow-wow," Marty said enthusiastically. "It was fun—and we learned a lot, too."

"We loved your bear dance, Marty," Sammy said. "When you become a big star in Hollywood, we'll tell everyone you got your start on the reserve."

"Powwows are unique to our people," the Chief said. "In colonial times, Indians held powwows and the Europeans who came here were delighted with them. They are named after a dancer named 'Pauwau.' The Europeans mistook his name for the name of the ceremony and they spelled it 'powwow.' You saw all of our young boys and girls wearing their regalia, learning traditional dances and celebrating our culture. Sometimes a powwow will bring old foes together in friendship. One Assiniboin told me, 'I come to the powwow to help others and to celebrate with others. I forget old grievances. I can be a real Indian again. I gain strength to carry on with my life.'"

Susan waved her fingers, signalling her desire to speak. When the old Chief nodded in her direction, she held up two pieces of paper. "Look!" she said. "These are the targets we were shooting at today. I took them down from the trees. Notice anything?"

Max said, "Yes, one bull's eye looks slightly larger than the other. How come?"

"It's those Bradleys," Susan said. "Caught cheating again. They made their bull's eye larger than ours. Not much larger, but still, it was an advantage. It's just another example of their dishonesty."

Chief Echo shook his head. "My old eyes did not notice," he sighed. "I fear the Bradleys are incorrigible."

Marty nudged Max and whispered, "What's that word mean?"

"It means they'll never reform. They'll always be cheaters."

"Chief, do you think the Bradleys will be prosecuted?" Max asked. "You know, for burning down the longhouse and for breaking other laws?"

"Not likely, Max. Not many judges or law enforcement people care much about the injustices done to our people. I doubt the Bradleys will be convicted of anything. Besides, the silver has run out from their mine and they will leave the area soon. Silver City will die and become a ghost town. Another mining town will spring up here—if we sell the mineral rights to this land. By then, we too will be gone, living peacefully in that beautiful valley ten miles up the road. We will be with Mother Nature and be at peace. If a man strays too far from nature, his voice becomes hard, his smile shrinks in his mouth, his ears do not hear the hoot of the owl, his eyes do not see the rabbit in his garden." He stopped and raised a finger. "By the way, we must think of a name for our new home."

"How about Lacrosseville?" Marty blurted out.

Everybody in the longhouse chuckled.

"No, we will give it a proper name. A new name for a new beginning. But something akin to Tumbling Waters.

"There's a stretch of rapids on the river up there," Max said. "How about Tumbling Rapids?"

"Very good, Max," said the Chief. "An excellent name. I will discuss it with my elders."

Marty reached out and patted his brother on the back.

"I thought one of you might ask what will happen to Elmo," the Chief said, smiling.

The others glanced at Elmo but said nothing. "I

have decided that Elmo deserves a chance to redeem himself," the Chief stated. "We have talked and Elmo agrees that he walked down a crooked path. But he has promised to stay on the straight path from now on. Susan will help him catch up on his schooling. Both Susan and I think he has much potential. And we all know he excels as an athlete."

Max saw Susan and Elmo exchange shy smiles.

Then Max said, "Why not try out for our hockey team next season, Elmo? Sammy joined us last season and became a star. Maybe you could be one, too."

Elmo's face lit up. "I'd love that, Max. Thanks for inviting me."

"But you can't play in goal," Marty said hastily. "That's my position."

"Don't worry. I'm a forward in hockey," Elmo said, drawing laughter and a sigh of relief from Marty.

Max looked at his watch. "My folks will be coming to pick us up soon. We're all packed and ready to go. But I wanted to say again how much we've enjoyed being in your village. I'm sure Marty and I will remember this experience for as long as we live."

The old Chief thanked Max for his compliment and winked at Sammy.

Sammy stood up and faced the Mitchell brothers.

"Max and Marty," he said solemnly. "You have become like brothers to us in the past few days. We appreciate all that you have done for us. The great Chief has asked me to speak to Marty first. He has decided that your tribal name, Puny Turtle, no longer describes you. He wants to rename you. He says that small birds fly around in a group and low to the ground, but the eagle—the eagle soars high over everybody and flies alone, alone and unafraid. So your new name is Bold Eagle."

Marty was thrilled. Bold Eagle! What a great name!

Susan stepped forward and presented Marty with an Indian headdress, fashioned out of eagle feathers. She fitted it on his head.

"I made it myself," she said shyly.

Marty impulsively reached out and gave her a hug.

"It's beautiful," he stammered. "And that was a bear hug, Susan. My specialty."

"And we have another headdress for you, Max," Susan said, placing one on his head. Max gave Susan a hug and a kiss on both cheeks. "Thank you," he whispered in her ear. "You are the best archer I've ever seen. And a friend for life, I hope."

Susan blushed. "I hope so, too, Max."

Sammy turned to Max. "Max, we are close friends and teammates. I will always cherish the bond that exists between us. I know your feelings toward the Iroquois people are sincere. You have displayed much courage and skill in the time you've been with us, and our people appreciate it. We have a gift for you and Marty—one you can share—but you will have to step outside the longhouse to see it."

Everybody rose and Sammy led the group outside. Max and Marty were stunned by what they saw. Quietly, the entire community had gathered around the huge fire. When Max and Marty appeared, there was a spontaneous round of applause. Someone began to beat on a drum and children started dancing around the fire. In a soft voice, Chief Echo said to the Mitchell brothers, "To our people, marching to a drum is like dancing to the heartbeat of Mother Earth."

Sammy called for silence.

From the crowd, two young men emerged, carrying a canoe.

"This is an authentic birch bark canoe," Sammy said with pride. "For decades, the canoe has been an important means of transportation for our people. This canoe, which Susan and I made with the Chief as our mentor, has wooden ribs, bent into shape after being soaked in hot water to soften them. It is covered by thick sheets of birch bark, which have been carefully sewn into place. The seams have been covered by white pine pitch and your names have been engraved on each side of the bow—Flying Hare and Bold Eagle. It's lightweight, portable and built for two. I must sound like a car salesman," Sammy added, laughing. "And if I were, now would be the time to present you with the keys. Instead, I present you with two handmade paddles. They are the keys to your new canoe."

Max and Marty accepted the paddles and raised them high in the air, a salute to all of their new friends. Max stepped forward to speak, looked over the faces and saw two that surprised him.

"Mom! Dad! When did you get here?"

"The Chief asked us to come up a little early, son," Harry Mitchell shouted. "He wanted us to see this presentation. We'll strap that canoe on the roof of the car a little later."

Max grinned, blew his mother a kiss and then turned to Chief Echo. "Thank you, Great Chief, for this wonderful gift. Whenever Marty and I are paddling across a lake, whenever we explore some stream or river, we will think of you. You are a very wise and generous chief. You have allowed us to live in your village. You have taught us much about your history and your culture. We thank you—and Sammy and Susan—for this amazing gift. We thank Susan for these headdresses, which we wear with pride. You are warm, wonderful, friendly people. Thank you once more."

Everyone cheered and applauded.

"Max and Marty," Sammy said, "we will all understand if you don't wear the headdresses to school, to church, or on the hockey rink. You might take quite a teasing. Save them until you come back and see us again. How about next summer?"

"Next summer for sure," Max and Marty said in unison.

Brian McFarlane, with 53 books to his credit, is one of Canada's most prolific authors of hockey books. He comes by his writing honestly, for he is the son of Leslie McFarlane, a.k.a. Franklin W. Dixon, author of the first 21 books in the Hardy Boys series. With his father in mind and with two brothers not unlike the Hardy Boys as his central characters, Brian has created a new fiction series for young readers—the Mitchell Brothers.

LOOKING AHEAD

When Max and Marty's parents decide to purchase some country property, the owner won't sell unless the Mitchells agree to take a mysterious horse called Wizard. It's all part of the deal. Reluctantly, Mr. Mitchell agrees and the purchase of Wizard triggers new adventures for the brothers, beginning with a friendship with Trudy Reeves, an outstanding teenage harness driver.

To the Mitchells' surprise, Trudy sees great potential in Wizard. But so do some scoundrels in the area. She and the Mitchell brothers are hard pressed to protect Wizard from horse thieves.

Sit back in the sulky for this one—*Wizard the Wonder Horse*—and hold on tight for another Mitchell brothers adventure.